When Delcie first bumped into Brad Bellamy it seemed like just another accident. Then she began to see that Fate intended them to get to know one another. But Amanda believed in making one's own destiny – and she made it clear that hers included Brad, too . . .

Books you will enjoy
by MIRIAM MACGREGOR

THE MALVERN MAN

Julie needed a holiday – so she went to stay with her cousin. Unfortunately her cousin worked for Adam Malvern – Julie's father's arch rival – and Adam was not too pleased to find her exercising his precious horses . . .

CALL OF THE MOUNTAIN

Lisa hadn't the slightest wish to renew her unsatisfactory relationship with Paul Mason – but how could she convince Brett Arlington of that? And why was it so important that she should?

WINTER AT WHITECLIFFS

Lindy needed the job at Whitecliffs as governess to little Danny. But Scott Wardell thought she was too young, and had no hesitation in telling her to go home. But when he changed his mind and agreed to give her a month's trial, Lindy wondered whether she was wise to stay on, especially with the beautiful Cheryl making her opinion only too obvious . . .

STAIRWAY TO DESTINY

BY
MIRIAM MACGREGOR

MILLS & BOON LIMITED
15–16 BROOK'S MEWS
LONDON W1A 1DR

*First published in Great Britain 1986
by Mills & Boon Limited*

© Miriam Macgregor 1986

*Australian copyright 1986
Philippine copyright 1987
This edition 1987*

ISBN 0 263 75584 3

*Set in Times 10 on 10¼ pt.
01-0287-54236*

*Computer typeset by SB Datagraphics,
Colchester, Essex*

*Printed and bound in Great Britain by
Collins, Glasgow*

CHAPTER ONE

THE strong breeze had developed into a howling gale, but that was not unusual in the city known as Windy Wellington. On that afternoon in late November when it was supposed to be summer, the sky was overcast and strong gusts whipped round corners. Pedestrians were forced to button coats and lower their heads as they made their way along streets.

People on higher levels of the hilly city were caught in the wind's full blast, although it seemed to have little impact on the students leaving the commercial college up near the university. It fanned Delcie's blonde hair across her face, causing her eyes to water, and as she made her way down the wide front steps she found herself jostled from behind by happy teenage girls who chatted gaily as they began their end-of-term freedom.

Although Delcie looked like a student she was in fact a teacher, and as she crossed the car park towards her small blue Honda Civic three of her pupils caught up with her.

'Cheerio, Miss Linden,' they chorused, then one of them added, 'We hope you have a really lovely holiday and a good rest.'

'Thank you.' She forced herself to smile at the trio. Did they honestly think she looked so worn out she needed a good rest?

'Don't think about any of us until next year,' advised the second girl as she pushed long wind-blown hair from her face.

'I'll practice on Dad's typewriter during the hols,' promised the third, although not very convincingly.

'You do that.' Delcie smiled again. Holidays indeed, she thought wistfully. How nice to be free to do as one wished.

The three friends watched as she unlocked the car door. 'Are you going away for the hols, Miss Linden?' one of them asked.

Miss Linden. These teenagers made her feel so much older than her twenty-three years. 'Yes, I'll be going somewhere or other,' she replied vaguely and without admitting that the destination would depend entirely upon the decisions made by Aunt Lois and Aunt Alice, with whom she lived.

Even now they'd be arguing about it. Aunt Lois was determined it would be Queenstown in the deep south, while Aunt Alice was doing her best to make it Bay of Islands in the far north. Not that she ever got anywhere when arguing with stubborn Aunt Lois.

The voice of the youngest girl cut across Delcie's thoughts. Her eyes shining with suppressed excitement, she said, 'My boy-friend is taking me on his father's yacht. We're going to Picton in the Marlborough Sounds. I hope this wretched wind drops before we sail, otherwise I'll be terribly seasick.'

'*My* boy-friend is taking me all the way to Dunedin,' one of the others said. 'I'm to meet his family,' she added shyly.

Boy-friends. How lucky they were, Delcie thought as she slid behind the wheel. How fortunate not to be living with aunts who frightened the living daylights out of every potential boy-friend who came near her. She frowned as she recalled inviting Sam to meet them. It had been his first and last visit; nor had he bothered to phone her again. And there had been Eric and Tony, who had been questioned extensively about their family background. It had been most embarrassing, and even now she cringed at the memory.

Later, when she had protested, it had been the same old story.

'My dear,' the aunts had echoed in unison, 'we're only trying to protect you. If your dear mother hadn't gone off with that fellow, she'd be alive today.' Whereupon two pairs of pale blue eyes had glared at her almost accusingly.

As usual their words had silenced Delcie, because they never failed to make her feel guilty. She had been born a year after her parents' runaway marriage. At the age of three she had become ill with whooping cough, and it had been while driving frantically to place his gasping little daughter in the hands of a doctor that her father had taken a hill bend too sharply. The car had rolled down a steep slope and while she herself had been thrown clear, her parents had been killed.

The fact that her father had also lost his life in the accident was never mentioned by the aunts. In their eyes he would always be looked upon as 'that fellow', and the less said about him, the better. However, when it had been discovered he had no relatives in New Zealand, it had been left to Miss Lois and Miss Alice Truscott to take their sister's child into their care.

Nor had Delcie been allowed to forget this fact, which appeared to be tied up with the duties she owed them. And over the years duty had become a favourite word with Aunt Lois. 'It's your *duty* to live with us, dear,' she had declared when Delcie had suggested moving into a flat of her own. 'We need your assistance, dear. We took you in when you became an orphan, and now it's your turn to help us.'

Aunt Alice had agreed, and as usual the pale blue eyes of both aunts had stared at her reproachfully.

'You don't really need my help,' Delcie had argued. 'You're both perfectly capable. After all, you're only in your fifties.'

Lois Truscott's voice had become cold. 'My dear, you know we never discuss our ages.'

Alice had blinked at Delcie in her usual pathetic manner. 'Don't you see, dear? It's not only your help in the house, and the fact that you do the meals at weekends, it's the financial assistance you give us——'

'Be quiet, Alice,' Lois had snapped, her eyes glinting as she added, 'I think we can rely on Delcie to understand where her duty lies. Now then, the subject is closed.'

A similar reaction had occurred when Delcie had hinted she had been thinking of taking her holiday with a friend who also taught at the commercial college. It was to have been at Ohope Beach where they would bask in the warm Bay of Plenty sunshine.

The aunts had been shocked. Rapid glances had passed between them and then Lois had exclaimed, 'But, my dear, we need you to help us with our suitcases, and the reservations, and everything.'

Alice had quavered, 'Surely you wouldn't let us down, or desert us? Suppose one of us became ill? You'd never forgive yourself,' she added slyly.

It was the trump card that had the desired result, and although the same discussion arose each year the argument always ended with Delcie's holiday being dominated by her aunts. Each vacation became more boring than the last, and this year the routine was about to be repeated. They would look at shops, walk in public gardens or sit in the motel. Excitement of any description for herself would be non-existent.

The thoughts swam through her head as the Honda Civic swung round the hilly corners rising towards the suburb of Karori, and perhaps it was a vision of the looming dull period that forced Aunt Lois's new dress into her mind. 'Blast!' she muttered under her breath as she slowed down and stopped the car at the kerbside.

The dress had been purchased in a shop on Lambton

Quay in the city. The hem had needed adjustment and the garment now waited to be collected. Delcie had been directed to do this, and she knew that Aunt Lois would be furious if she went home without it. She also knew she had no option but to drive back to the city, so she made a swift U-turn and within minutes the Honda was nosing its way downhill, negotiating corners until it reached the street known as The Terrace which lay along the rise above Lambton Quay.

She guessed that parking in the city would be difficult to find, so when a space between the cars lining The Terrace caught her eye she slid into it gratefully. Fortunately it was near a lengthy flight of steps that would take her down to the quay, and as she crossed the road towards them, the high buildings acted as a funnel for the violent wind that billowed her skirt and jacket.

A second funnel was formed by the steps as they descended between buildings, and she was hastening down them, when strong gusts caused thick clouds of dust to swirl about her feet. Some of it rose to find its way into her eyes. She gave a cry as the pain caused by grit brought her to an abrupt halt and, almost completely blinded, she stood blinking for several moments while her eyes watered and stung.

At last, with her eyes only partly open, she tried to hasten on her way, but through discomfort and her lowered head she failed to see the man coming up the steps. He, too, had his head lowered, and the collision occurred on the corner where the steps turned to the right. The force of the impact sent them both off balance. His arm was flung out as he fell sprawling, and as Delcie landed heavily with her knee upon his hand her weight jammed it against the hard concrete step.

The man swore and gave a sudden yelp of acute pain. 'Dammit! Get off my hand, you—you stupid *female*.' The word came out like an insult.

The breath had been knocked out of Delcie and, shocked by the unexpectedness of the fall, she had been momentarily immobilised. However, she now struggled to her feet, being vaguely conscious of the stinging pain of skinned knees.

'I'm sorry—I'm so sorry,' she gasped, feeling sure the fault had been hers. She shouldn't have been scrambling down the steps with her eyes half closed, she told herself. If only she'd remembered the dress when leaving the college she wouldn't have bumped into this man at this precise moment.

The man in question sat on the step, rocking himself as though in agony while he held his hand against his chest. 'Why the hell couldn't you watch where you you were going?' he snarled. 'You were well over on this side of the steps. Don't you know to keep to the left? Or is that too much to expect?'

'I'm afraid I had dust in my eyes,' she faltered. 'I've said I'm sorry.'

'I should damned well think so,' he gritted, his face white and drawn from pain.

'It takes two to collide,' she retorted. 'You weren't keeping much account of where *you* were going. It's not *all* my fault.' She stared at his hand and then at the obvious distress in the brown eyes beneath the dark brows. 'Does your hand hurt?' she ventured timidly.

'You can bet your life it does. My entire arm is one big ache,' he lashed at her through clenched teeth.

'I'm afraid your hand looks as if it's swelling.'

'Really? How very observant,' he sneered. 'Of course it's swelling. It's coming up like a balloon!'

'Do you think something's broken?' she ventured nervously.

'I've a strong suspicion about it.' He winced as he tried to move his fingers. 'What on earth do I do now?'

She was gripped by remorse. 'I'm afraid it's my fault——'

'You can say that again,' he snapped. 'You're not very big but the force of your weight coming down on my hand on the concrete step has certainly done something serious.'

'It's your right hand,' she began, then fell silent as her mind conjured the extra problems this fact could add.

'Yes, it's my right hand,' he added wearily. 'You're being observant again.'

She ignored the irony behind the last words. 'Please, let me do something for you.'

'Do something? Haven't you done enough?' he demanded scathingly.

She became impatient with him. 'I've explained my eyes were filled with dust. They were hurting—I could hardly see where I was going. Now then, do you want me to help you, or not?'

'I'm afraid I'm going to need help from somebody,' he admitted reluctantly.

'Very well.' She became practical. 'Personally I think your hand should be examined by a doctor, and the sooner the better. Have you a car parked somewhere?'

He shook his head. 'No, I don't usually bring a car to Wellington.' Then, frowning, he stared at his rapidly swelling hand. 'Hell's teeth—I've never felt anything like this before!'

Delcie said, 'I've a car on The Terrace. If I take you to a doctor you might have to sit for ages in his waiting room. I think the best plan would be to take you straight to the accident or casualty department at the public hospital. I feel sure an X-ray will be necessary.'

He stood up nursing his hand and again wincing with pain. It was then she realised he was a tall man with more than his share of good looks. His straight dark hair was thick, while his firm jaw stamped him as a man of determination. She placed his age at about thirty and, while his clothes were well-cut garments normally worn in the city, a vague ruggedness stamped him as an outdoor man. Perhaps it was his tanned complexion or the tiny white lines about his brown eyes, caused by squinting against the sun.

She tried to carry his briefcase as they mounted the steps to The Terrace, but he snatched at it with his left hand. 'I'm not entirely helpless,' he snarled at her.

At last she had him in the car, and, watching his expression as they left the kerbside, she knew he continued to be in pain. The traffic lights were kind as they reached the lower end of The Terrace, and then they drove through the city towards Newtown where the hospital was situated. He remained silent as they found their way to Casualty where they were obliged to sit and wait, but eventually he was led away by a white-coated attendant.

Delcie continued to sit and wait. She realised she could now leave him because he was in capable hands, and after his injury had received attention a taxi would take him to wherever he wished to go. Yet something stronger than herself kept her glued to the seat. It would be like running away, she decided.

She glanced at her watch several times as the minutes ticked by slowly. No doubt he was in the X-ray department, she told herself, and then, just as she was wondering if he would have to remain overnight, he returned to her, his face grim.

The sight of his right hand set in plaster and held by a sling caused her to utter a small cry as she stood up to face him. 'Is it broken?' she whispered at last.

He glared at her furiously. 'Do you imagine the damned thing's in plaster for a joke?'

She was so full of remorse she was near tears. 'I'm—I'm so very sorry,' was all she could say.

Scowling at her, he snapped, 'I'm surprised to find you still here. I was sure you'd have vanished.'

His words wiped some of her pity away. 'Of course I'm still here. Did you expect me to leave you?'

'To be honest, I didn't know what to expect.'

'Besides, your briefcase is still in the car. Did you think I'd go off with it—that I'd *steal* it?'

He ignored the remark, his scowl becoming darker as another problem appeared to leap into his mind. 'My briefcase—damnation! This'll put paid to that for today.'

'Is there anything I can do to help?' What was in the briefcase? she wondered.

He shook his head. 'It'll have to wait.'

'I've said I'll help you,' she persisted. 'I'll do anything to help you. You'll need to be driven somewhere.' Guilt was growing steadily, consuming her like a glowing flame as she looked at the hanging empty sleeve of his expensive suede jacket.

'*Help*! You can put a ring round that statement. Look at it, will you. Just take a damned good look at it.' He almost shoved the injured hand at her.

She stared at the white plaster which came down to cover his fingertips, and it was then she realised he was more than angry—he was *livid*. Quailing beneath his glare, she stammered, 'I—I can only repeat—I'm so—so very sorry.'

'So you said before, but a fat lot of good it'll do me,' he snapped. 'Being sorry won't get me out of the mess I'm in now.'

As they made their way towards the car park Delcie was at a loss for words apart from a nervous question. 'Can I drive you home or—or somewhere?'

His mouth twisted slightly. 'To drive me home would mean a trip of more than sixty miles into the Wairarapa district. My farm lies a few miles out of Masterton, but tonight I'm staying at the Town House Hotel in Oriental

Bay. Do you think you can find your way to Oriental Bay without bumping into anything?' His voice rang with bitter sarcasm.

She swung round to face him, her anger rising to match his own. 'Can't you understand it was an accident? If it hadn't been necessary to collect Aunt Lois's dress it would never have happened.'

'Nice to have something else to blame,' he sneered.

'You could've bumped into someone who would have gone off and left you,' she argued. 'I'm beginning to be sorry I didn't.'

'Are you, indeed?' His tone was curt.

'Yes, I am,' she snapped. 'Next time I'll run.'

'You won't, you know. You're not the type.'

She refrained from pointing out that he didn't know what type she happened to be, and they drove in silence as the car left Newtown and later turned on to Oriental Parade. The wide expanse of busy harbour now lay on their left, while on their right houses covered the hillside.

Delcie watched for the opening which gave access to the Town House Hotel and, driving up the rise, she parked near the entrance. She had known exactly where to go because Sam had taken her there before that disastrous evening when she had invited him home to meet the aunts.

The man beside her said, 'I see you know your way here.'

'Yes, I was brought here for a meal,' she returned briefly.

'Then perhaps you'll be good enough to join me for a meal this evening. As you can see, I'll need someone to cut my meat.'

'You're certainly demanding your pound of flesh,' she retorted. 'And that's not meant to be a pun.'

'You don't consider you owe me that much? You'd find difficulty in eating with me?'

It's your attitude I find difficult to stomach,' she flashed at him. 'You're a bore who's terribly sorry for himself.'

'Don't you think I've a right to be sorry for myself? How do you think I'll manage about my daily shower, or tying my shoe laces?'

'You'll have to find yourself a valet,' she said sweetly.

'Or a handmaiden,' he cut in.

'You can wear a plastic cover over your plaster,' she added hastily. 'As for shoes, you can wear the slip-on type.'

He gave a short laugh. 'You certainly have all the answers, but actually they're not the worst of my problems.'

'Oh?' She fell silent, afraid to ask about further problems.

'Come into the hotel and you'll see for yourself,' he suggested.

'I'll have to phone my aunts,' she said. 'They'll be wondering why I haven't arrived home.'

'You can do that from my room,' he told her as he led the way through the foyer towards a lift.

His room? She looked at him doubtfully. Did he have further demands in mind? Her thoughts returned to the aunts, her own mind in a whirl as she sorted out an explanation to be given to Aunt Lois, who would be sure to answer the phone. And this, she realised, might prove to be difficult, because as yet she didn't even know his name.

'Dinner at the Town House?' Aunt Lois would boom. 'With whom, may I ask?' 'Oh—just someone I bumped into,' she would reply. Never had she been invited to dinner under such strange circumstances, and she decided to make as little explanation as possible. When she reached home would be soon enough to face that particular hassle.

She brushed the problem aside as she entered his suite, which consisted of a bedroom, toilet facilities and a small lounge overlooking the harbour. But it was not the panoramic view of sparkling waters edged by the city and hills beyond the tall buildings that caught her attention, it was the sight of a portable typewriter with a stack of neatly typed sheets beside it.

She turned surprised eyes upon him. 'Is this a—a manuscript of some kind?'

'It is.' His tone was terse.

She was puzzled. 'But—didn't you say you're a farmer?'

'I happen to own a farm. I'm also a writer.'

'You're writing a book?'

'I am. Or should I say, I *was*?'

It was then that the full seriousness of his injury really hit her. 'You won't be able to type,' she said quietly. 'This is your main problem?'

He looked at her mockingly. 'You've noticed? And please don't say you're sorry again. I've been given that particular message—for what it's worth.' The words whipped her as his frustration made itself evident.

She looked at him in silence, her mind grasping the situation. He's a strong, masterful man, she thought. Suddenly he's been put out of action—and I've done this to him. No wonder he's infuriated with me. Nevertheless her chin rose as she said, 'I can understand that you hate the sight of me. However, I think you're a sarcastic devil. Thank you for your offer of a meal, but I'd prefer to go home. The waiter can cut your meat, or you can order a fork meal.'

She swung round and was almost to the door when his left hand shot out to grab her arm and spin her round to face him.

'Just a minute,' he rasped. 'Surely you can be gracious enough to join me in a drink. Heaven knows I need it, and perhaps you could do with a little pick-me-up as well.'

She returned his gaze defiantly, her blue eyes wide as they reflected the deep turquoise of her coat. 'Gracious? I know who's being most ungracious.'

He ignored the accusation as he took iced water from a small fridge in the corner of the lounge. 'What would you like? Scotch, sherry, or a gin and lemon squash?'

'A very small gin with lemon squash and water, thank you.' She felt she needed something to help her cope with this situation—something to give her extra strength and confidence.

He began to fumble with the screw top of the bottle. She took it from him, but he snatched it back. 'No, let me do it.' Then, sitting down, he held the bottle firmly between his knees while he unscrewed the top, following this with several other bottles. 'There, now, I'm not so helpless after all,' he grinned as he poured himself a double Scotch.

'I can see you're a determined man.'

'So I'm told by those who come up against me.'

The grin had changed his entire expression, lifting the anger from his face and making her realise he was even more handsome than she had at first thought. He had good teeth and his mouth had lines of humour about it. However, his next words recalled the situation.

'Weren't you going to ring an aunt, or somebody?'

'Oh, yes. I suppose I'd better do that.'

'And you will have dinner with me, please?'

She capitulated. 'Very well, but I don't even know your name.'

'Brad Bellamy. And your name?' The brown eyes swept over her slim form.

'Delcie Linden.' It seemed a strange introduction, she thought.

'I haven't asked how you fared in that fall on the stairs. You didn't appear to be hurt.'

She shrugged away the question. 'Only torn nylons and a couple of skinned knees.' She lifted her skirt to examine the raw patches upon which the blood had now congealed.

He looked at them, frowning until he said, 'You didn't say a word about them.'

'It was so little in comparison——' She became silent as she shied away from pointing out that by falling on him she had come off lightly. Then, noticing him give a sudden wince of pain, she felt compelled to ask, 'Does it hurt much?'

His mouth twisted slightly. 'You can believe I know it's there, even if I've been given pills to help me along the way.' He nodded towards the phone. 'There it is. Make your call.'

She resented his tone. 'Are you ordering me?'

'Yes. Otherwise you might slip through the door and run away.'

'I'd have thought you'd be anxious to see the back of me.'

'Strangely, I'm not.'

'Sitting opposite you at dinner, I'll continue to be a ghastly reminder of—of what's happened to your hand.'

'On the contrary, I'm expecting scintillating conversation to take my mind off the pain.'

'From me? With that plaster and sling staring me in the face? You've got to be joking! Or are you deliberately trying to punish me by forcing me to take a good look at what I've done?'

'I said, there's the phone.' His voice had become harsh.

She dialled the number reluctantly, and, as she had expected, the receiver was lifted by Aunt Lois, who always seemed to reach the phone first. The strong voice rang with irritation as it echoed over the line for all the world to hear.

'Delcie, where are you? We've been so worried. You should've been home ages ago.'

'I'm afraid I can't explain just now, Aunt. I'm ringing to let you know I'm having dinner with—with a—a person I've met.'

'Are you indeed? Who is this person, may I ask?'

'You—you don't know him, Aunt.'

'I hope you're not doing anything foolish, Delcie.' Lois Truscott's voice offered a dire warning.

'I'm not a child, Aunt Lois,' Delcie said stiffly.

'Hmm, well, I'm not so sure about that.' There was a pause and then the dominating tones continued to ring through clearly. 'I hope you collected my new dress from Kirk's?'

'No, I'm sorry. I'm afraid I was unable to do so.'

'Delcie, are you saying you failed to collect my new dress? How could you be so forgetful when you know I expected you to bring it home?' Anger now boomed through the phone.

Delcie could almost see the steely glitter in her aunt's pale blue eyes. 'I'm sorry, Aunt Lois. I'll collect it for you on Monday——'

'Really, Delcie, I'm very disappointed in you. I trust you don't intend to come creeping in too late this evening.'

'No, Aunt, I'll not be late,' she promised, then, replacing the receiver, she was filled with acute embarrassment because, as usual, Aunt Lois had succeeded in making her feel like a half-witted child.

She also knew that the raised voice had been clearly heard by Brad Bellamy. During the telephone conversation he had poured himself another double Scotch which he carried to the window where he now stood with his back to her.

'Trouble in the home camp?' he asked without turning his head.

She gave a faint smile. 'Aunt Lois is not amused. I suppose you could hear it all?'

'Every word. A bit of a tyrant, is she?'

'Well—she certainly rules the roost.'

'I think you could do with another drink.' He poured it deftly with his left hand, and as he passed it to her he added grimly, 'You can't fly on one wing—although some of us have to.'

'You're determined I'll not forget,' she snapped.

Sipping his Scotch, Brad stared across the harbour towards lights that were beginning to prick the early evening. 'Sit down and tell me about Aunt Lois,' he demanded.

'How can she possibly interest you?'

'I'm curious. Why does she frighten you? You don't impress me as being one who is easily scared.'

'She does *not* frighten me,' Delcie denied indignantly.

'Rubbish. Your fear quaked out of your voice. It came through clearly. Why do you live with her? A girl of your age should have her own flat.'

'It's—it's something to do with duty,' she admitted miserably. 'Aunt Alice agrees with her.'

'Aunt Alice? She's there, too?'

'She's a little younger and more gentle than Aunt Lois, although there are odd occasions when she actually tries to assert herself, like—like the present argument that's going on.'

'Oh? What's that about?'

The gin was beginning to make Delcie feel more relaxed, and as she was not in the habit of drinking alcohol, it was also loosening her tongue as she explained the problem of this year's holiday.

'Why is it your duty to go with them?' he queried.

'Surely it's your opportunity to give yourself a break from them.'

'They declare they need my help with this, that and the other. They're my mother's sisters. When my parents died in a car accident they took me under their wings. It's my duty to repay them.' The words came mechanically. They had been instilled so repeatedly by Aunt Lois that they were now part of Delcie's automatic thinking.

'What you're really saying is that they have a hold on you—a permanent assistant on tap—and they don't intend to let you go.'

'Not quite. I do go to a job each day,' she defended.

'Nevertheless, you'll be a great comfort in their old age,' he hinted with a wry smile.

There had been times when Delcie herself had realised this fact, but loyalty kept her silent. After all, the aunts had taken her into their home.

'How old are you?' The question came abruptly.

'Twenty-three,' she whispered as though ashamed of the fact.

'I see no engagement ring. Have you a boy-friend?'

She shook her head miserably. Boy-friend? Huh!

'I'll bet Aunt Lois attends to each one with the subtle charm of a dragon,' he remarked shrewdly.

Again loyalty made her refrain from admitting the truth. Instead, in an effort to change the subject, she said, 'I think I've told you enough about my affairs. Tell me about your book. I'm sure it's much more interesting. Is it fiction or non-fiction?'

'Non-fiction. It's about dogs.'

'*Dogs*?' She was unable to disguise her surprise.

'Sheepdogs are the real stars in it. As I mentioned earlier, I have a farm, but I didn't explain that it's managed for me while I indulge in my literary hobby.'

'You're married, of course,' she said, assuming this to

be a fact, yet wondering why the question should interest her.

'Definitely not,' he said firmly as he topped their half-empty glasses. 'Nor am I engaged, although Mother is doing her best to rectify that state of affairs.'

She did not wish to appear curious but was unable to resist a question. 'You live with your mother?'

'Yes, or perhaps I should say that Mother lives with me.'

'Oh?' She fell silent, waiting for him to say more, and, watching as he sipped his drink, she knew the Scotch was relaxing him even as the gin and squash had calmed her own nerves. 'Tell me about the farm,' she urged, without admitting to herself that she'd like to know more about this man.

'It's not one that's been in the family for generations,' he said. 'It was purchased by my grandfather and managed for him by my father until Dad died after being thrown from a horse.'

'Oh, I'm sorry——'

'A few years ago I inherited the property under my grandfather's will. It's known as Bellairs.'

'That's a nice name for a Bellamy property.'

'Grandfather decided upon it. He was searching for a name when one of his old mates teasingly suggested that, as a new owner of five thousand acres, he'd be putting on airs. Grandmother was indignant, but Grandfather laughed, and with his particular sense of humour he declared that there was the name of the property—Bellairs.'

His previous words swam into her mind. 'What did you mean when you said your mother was doing her best?'

'Oh, well, I've long since become used to the fact that she'd like to see me settled with the girl next door. Her name's Amanda Stafford,' he admitted gruffly.

'Amanda? She's pretty?' She was politely interested.

'Her arrival goes back about fifteen years to when we had a disastrous farming patch. There were heavy financial losses after bad cattle deals, and then the ewes were struck by a disease known as facial eczema, caused by a liver complaint. These tremendous setbacks knocked hell out of everything, forcing us to sell one half of the property to consolidate the other half. It means that Bellairs is no longer five thousand acres—it's down to two thousand, five hundred.'

'Are you saying that half of Bellairs was sold to Amanda's parents?' she asked, working out the situation for herself.

'Yes, but at least Edgar Stafford's a good farmer.'

'Am I right in assuming she's an only child?'

'You are. So what?' he demanded curtly.

Delcie gave a sudden laugh. 'The rest is easy to guess. Marry Amanda and eventually the property will be joined again. I can understand how your mother feels about it. Why don't you tie the knot and make her happy?'

'Because I do not intend to be bullied into marriage for the sake of a lump of land,' he snarled angrily. 'Nor can I understand why the devil I'm confiding these private affairs to one who has inconvenienced me so much.' He almost spat the words at her.

CHAPTER TWO

HE was still furious with her, she realised, but the glass in her hand had helped to keep her own mood cheerful. 'It's good to talk about problems,' she pointed out. 'Perhaps another Scotch will put you into a more mellowed state. You might even find yourself forgiving me.'

'That's unlikely,' Brad retorted. 'Can't you see what you've done? You've put me in Mother's hands completely.'

She giggled. 'No doubt she'll call in Amanda at once. They'll both be waiting on you hand and foot.'

'You're darned right, although I don't suppose that'll be so bad. Amanda will probably drive me to the doctor for a painkiller prescription.

Irritated for some unknown reason, she snapped, 'Please don't hesitate to send his account to me.'

'It might be costly,' he warned drily.

'I don't care,' she retorted, her chin rising. 'I can pay for it. I told you I have a job, didn't I?'

'So you did. What sort of job is it? Are you selling buttons and lace to old ladies?'

'*No, I am not,*' she said, her colour rising at his obvious low regard for her capabilities. 'I teach typing in a commercial college,' she informed him loftily.

'You—teach typing?' He looked at her thoughtfully, his eyes slightly narrowed as he digested this fact.

'I said so, didn't I?' She put her glass down carefully then crossed the room to where his pile of typing paper rested beside the typewriter. A pen lay nearby and, scribbling on the top blank sheet, she said, 'There you are, that's my home address. You can send your doctor's bill to me.'

He ignored her action as he said, 'I presume the college is closed for the year, and that fact enables you to go on holiday with the aunts.'

'That's the situation exactly.' She sat down again and sipped her drink.

He looked at her with an amused glint in his eyes. 'Speaking of your aunts, what would be their reaction if they could see you drinking gin with a stranger—and in his hotel bedroom?'

'They'd consider I'm being most indiscreet,' she admitted. 'Aunt Lois would rise in the air with horror.'

'And Aunt Alice?'

'She'd come over faint and feel quite dizzy. I'm afraid they're both rather allergic to male company.'

'Your mother must have been very different from her sisters.'

'She was much younger—what's known as an after-thought in her parents' lives. She married against the advice and wishes of her sisters—well, Lois's wishes, really, I suppose.'

'And these two harpies have had the handling of your young life?'

Loyalty forced her to say, 'They're not harpies. They've done their best for me—according to their lights.'

'Lights? Their lights must be very dim. No more than a flicker.'

Thoughts of the aunts and their disapproval caused her to glance at her watch. 'If we don't go to the dining-room soon I—I'll have to go home. In any case, it's time you had a meal.'

'You're afraid of them,' he jeered.

'I find it easier to comply with their wishes,' she

admitted reluctantly. 'It's all a matter of keeping the peace.'

'They've certainly got you by the ears,' he snorted. 'You'll end up by being exactly like them—an old maid.'

The derision in his voice echoed in her ears as she followed him to the dining-room. But no doubt he was right, she thought with a wave of misery and self-pity. She'd end up by being exactly like the aunts. Nor was anyone likely to rescue her from this fate.

She brushed the depressing thoughts aside as they were led to a table beside the windows. In keeping with the rest of the hotel, the Town House dining-room had its own vista of harbour and lights which now made a brilliant display in the darkness. Delcie found the scene breathtaking, but found difficulty in recognising it as the same Wellington she knew by daylight.

They were handed menus. Brad Bellamy ordered steak and then beckoned for a wine waiter.

Steak, Delcie thought. He really does intend that I'll cut his meat for him. But when it arrived it had already been sliced into bite-sized pieces.

The waiter spoke with an easy familiarity. 'You weren't wearing that plaster at lunchtime, Mr Bellamy. You've come up against something tough since then?'

'You might say so,' Brad informed him blandly. 'It has blonde hair and big blue eyes.'

The waiter swept an appreciative glance over Delcie who had turned scarlet. 'Knocked you sideways, did she?'

'That's about the situation. Thank you for cutting my meat.'

Delcie ignored the reference to herself but, as the waiter left the table, she remarked icily, 'They appear to know you in this place. One of their regulars, are you?'

'Yes. I always stay here when I visit Wellington.'

'You come to the city frequently?' She tried to sound casual.

'Only when I feel the need for a chat with my publisher.'

'Oh.' She looked at him thoughtfully. Would she ever see him again? she wondered. No, it was most unlikely. The vision of Aunt Lois already planted in his mind would be enough to make him think twice about getting in touch with her. And apart from that, he could only look upon her as someone who had caused him pain and inconvenience.

There was also that echo of derision in his voice when they had left his suite. It had amounted to contempt for one who lived as she was living—a poor pathetic thing who allowed herself to be dominated by a couple of elderly women. And hadn't he already suggested that she'd grow more like them every day?

A wave of depression hit her, but she pulled herself together sufficiently to indicate the sliced steak on his plate. 'You see, you didn't need my assistance after all.'

The brown eyes looked at her steadily, examining her features one by one, and although she waited for him to speak he said nothing.

Slightly embarrassed by his close scrutiny, she said hastily, 'Tell me about your book. Dogs, you said?'

'That's right. It's a mixture of history, anecdotes and stories about man's best friend. The publisher expects to see it on his desk by the end of February. At least that's the deadline according to my signed contract with him.'

'Contract?' She was startled. 'How far have you progressed with it?'

'I'm only about half-way through the manuscript. I've already gathered material from the South Island and from the north of the North Island. The aim is to give it an all-over New Zealand coverage, you understand.'

She nodded. 'I think so. What I can't understand is

why it must be finished by the end of February.'

'It's important to get it through its various stages of typesetting, proof-reading and printing so that it can be in the shops before the Christmas trading begins. You can say it's a matter of economics.' He paused, his expression changing as he glared at her furiously. 'Now do you understand what a mess I'm in? I'm in the position of having to break my contract with the publishers.'

The harshness of his last words startled her, making her realise that what appeared to be a mellowed attitude was merely a veneer. Beneath it he was still livid with her.

'Yes, I can see only too well,' she admitted miserably, then, as another thought struck her, 'What about driving a car? Have you a car here?'

'No, I don't bring my car to Wellington. It's easier to come by rail and use taxis when I'm here. It eliminates the hassle of parking meters that are so apt to expire.'

'So, when shall you go home?'

'Tomorrow, I suppose. I'll give Broadcasting a miss or simply post the scripts.'

Her eyes widened. 'Broadcasting?'

'I've compiled a couple of educational talks to be broadcast to schools. On dogs, of course. I'd intended to leave them at one of their offices on The Terrace and was on my way there when—we met.'

'You mean when *I* bumped into *you*. Why don't you say it?'

'Let's not discuss it.'

They ate in silence while Delcie's spirits sank to an even lower level as she realised he'd be going home tomorrow and that it was unlikely she'd ever see him again. Not that he'd want to see her again, of course. That would be most unlikely. But after all, why should she want to see him again? This had been an upsetting incident and perhaps better forgotten. Still, it was a pity.

Nor did she think Aunt Lois would succeed in making mincemeat of this man quite as easily as she'd churned up other young men who had come to take her out. That hard line of jaw denoted real stubbornness, she decided. Oh well, so be it. A sigh escaped her.

'What's the matter?' he demanded. 'Is your food not to your liking? Meat tough, or something?'

'Oh no, it's all delicious.'

'Then why the sigh?'

'I—I feel so ghastly about the whole situation. I'm worried for you, and I can only hope that, somehow, you'll finish the book in time to meet your deadline.'

'There's no hope of that now, I'm afraid.' Then, looking at her mockingly, 'One would almost imagine that you cared about it.'

'I do. Please believe me, I do.'

Brad shrugged in a resigned manner. 'I still have people to interview. There's a man at Otaki who expects to see me quite soon.'

'Otaki is miles away from Masterton, but no doubt Amanda will be able to drive you there.'

'Perhaps.' His tone was non-committal.

Why should the thought of Amanda irritate her? wondered Delcie. Or was her mind slightly jumbled through a little too much gin? 'She'll be able to take notes for you,' she said with forced brightness.

'I don't take notes. I persuade people to talk beside a tape recorder. Later it has to be listened to and the entire tape written down. Then it has to be edited into publishable form. It's quite a long task.'

She looked at his right hand and said nothing until, to break the awkward silence, she asked, 'Is there very much to write about dogs?' She regretted the question the moment it had left her tongue. Of course, there must be plenty—otherwise he wouldn't be writing a book about the animals.

He regarded her with weary toleration, giving her the impression he was too tired to be irritated by her stupidity, but at last he said, 'The subject covers a wide field. Every dog owner has a story about his pet, past or present, and apart from the amazing ability of sheepdogs there are the police dogs and the seeing-eye dogs for the blind. Have you ever owned a dog?' The question came abruptly.

'No. I'm afraid Aunt Lois——'

'Doesn't like dogs. That, I can imagine.'

'The city is not a good place for the type of dog I'd like to own,' Delcie defended. 'He'd need freedom for exercise.'

'Oh? And what type is that, may I ask?'

'A golden Labrador,' she admitted wistfully.

'I'm amazed that you can even name one breed.'

'I'll ignore that slur on my general knowledge, Mr Bellamy. I can understand you must be feeling completely worn out.'

'Flogged, is the word.'

'You should be in——' She paused, hesitating to finish the sentence which he might take as a suggestion or, worse still, as an invitation.

His eyes held amused speculation. 'As soon as we've had coffee in the lounge I'll be glad of your assistance to put me there.'

She almost choked, then decided he must be joking. 'One of the waiters will help you, or—or a member of staff,' she smiled.

'They're all on duty. Evening is a busy time for everyone. You won't object to helping me get my shirt off? Aunt Lois need never know,' he chuckled.

The glint beneath the lowered lids indicated he considered her to be a pathetic prude, and, pride coming to her rescue, she retorted coldly, 'Of course I'll help you. I'll see you right into bed.' The shock of her own words silenced her. Lord, what on earth was she saying?

'Good. I hoped you wouldn't see me stuck.'

A short time later they moved into the lounge where people sat round small tables or reclined in easy chairs, and as Delcie sipped her coffee she told herself she was being a fool. There'd be no great hassle in helping him undress. If she'd taken up nursing as a career she'd be undressing men who were strangers every day. The average girl would take this situation in her stride, but then the average girl hadn't been brought up by Aunt Lois, who considered all men to be first cousins to the devil.

His voice startled her as he leaned forward and spoke in low tones. 'Your face is full of apprehension. Are you afraid of me?'

'With that plaster on your hand? Certainly not,' she declared with an aloof air.

'That's a pity. It would boost my ego if I thought you feared me—even with one wing clipped.'

She looked at him thoughtfully, her deep blue eyes shadowed. There it was again, the subtle reminder of what she'd done to him. 'You're so very determined I'll not forget the—the damage I've caused, aren't you, Mr Bellamy? You needn't worry. This episode will remain with me for a long, long time.'

'Neither of us will forget it in a hurry,' he informed her gravely. 'So if you've finished that coffee we'll return to my rooms.'

She drained her cup hastily, and as she stood up she was gripped by a mad desire to run, until she recalled that her coat was still in his suite. When they reached it the galaxy of lights again drew her to the window, but somehow they had lost their fascination.

Moments later he was beside her, another glass of

Scotch in his hand. He sipped it in silence.

She glanced at him. 'Do you always drink so much?'

'Only when I've been winged,' he grinned. 'It's an excuse.'

'There you go again,' she snapped.

'Oh, yes. I forgot you take umbrage at being reminded—but this is helping me a little, you know.'

'I suppose so,' she admitted with sudden understanding.

He stood quietly finishing the drink, then left her to go to the bathroom. Moments later she heard him return and move about the room, but hadn't the courage to look round to see what he was doing.

Then his voice came from behind her. 'I can manage my shoes and socks, thank you.'

The tone was particularly polite and Delcie had a sudden suspicion he was laughing at her. He's a beast, she decided, but common sense told her to get the job over and be done with it.

When she turned to face him he had discarded his jacket which now lay on the floor. She picked it up and hung it in the wardrobe. He then stood like an obedient child waiting while she unbuttoned his shirt and drew it from his left arm and over the plaster. His vest was then eased over his head while he bent forward, although she felt quite sure he could have discarded it himself.

She also knew that he fumbled with his left hand, but was unprepared for his trousers to drop about his ankles. A small gasp escaped her and she knew she'd turned crimson at the sight of him standing in briefs alone. Her eyes became riveted on the lines of rippling muscles, the crispness of short dark hairs on his chest, then slid down his torso to the flatness of his stomach.

'You've never seen a man's body before, Miss Linden?' he asked smoothly.

She swallowed. 'Of course I have—in films, at the beach——'

'But not at such close quarters?'

She ignored the question. 'Where are your pyjamas?' Her voice came unsteadily and she cursed herself for being a fool.

'In the wardrobe, or under my pillow. I'll just wear the jacket if you'll be good enough to button it round me.'

As she searched for the pyjamas she became aware that her pulses had quickened and that her cheeks were still flushed. And when she returned with the garment she found it almost impossible to look at him. She also knew he was gazing at her through slits of eyes, and when his next words came they shocked her.

'I believe you're a virgin, Miss Linden.'

'So what?' she gasped angrily.

'They're few and far between these days, or so I'm told.'

She ignored the remark as she guided his left arm into the sleeve, then pulled the jacket around him and fastened the buttons.

His voice was low as he said, 'Thank you, Miss Linden, it's been nice knowing you. Under different circumstances I'd have been delighted to make your acquaintance.'

'Ditto, Mr Bellamy,' was all she could find to say, although she was aware that his eyes were holding her own with some sort of magnetic force she found hard to break.

And then the unexpected happened. His left arm, surprising with its strength, shot round her waist and dragged her against his side. The breath was almost knocked out of her as, startled, she could only gaze up at him speechlessly, her eyes like round sapphires.

But the pause was only momentary before his mouth came down upon her own softly parted lips in a kiss that sent Delcie's heart thudding up into her throat. Although it wasn't a long kiss, it was enough to tell her that this man was finding it necessary to keep himself under control, and, while she knew she should push him away, she had neither the strength nor the desire to do so. The essence of his masculinity seemed to wrap itself about her, enfolding her in a cloak of helplessness from which she was unable to escape.

At last, when the kiss ended, he continued to stare down into her face as though committing every feature to memory.

She stared back at him. 'You shouldn't have done that, Mr Bellamy. You had no right——'

'Opportunity is something to be grabbed, especially if it comes only once.'

'I think you're a little drunk.'

He laughed. 'Drunk? Me? That'll be the day. You'd better have one more kiss for the road, Miss Linden.' His left arm tightened about her again as his hard mouth returned to her lips. But suddenly he released her. 'Goodbye, Miss Linden.' His voice was gruff.

'Goodbye, Mr Bellamy,' she whispered, then, snatching up her coat and handbag, she fled from the room.

It was ages since Delcie had been kissed by a man, and the experience made her feel almost giddy. Exuberance caused her to watch her speed as she drove round the waterfront to where the road turned up towards the hilly suburb of Kelburn, and then beyond it to Karori.

On reaching home she had expected to find the house in darkness because the aunts usually retired early, but as she turned into the drive the lights in the house told her they were still up and waiting for her. She entered the lounge to find them sitting like a pair of judges who were about to sum up the question of whether or not she was guilty of some heinous crime. However, it was a situation to which she was accustomed.

Aunt Lois began the attack. She was of heavier build than Aunt Alice and always took the lead by divine right of seniority. She forced a smile as Delcie came into the room, but it carried little sign of a cheery welcome.

'Ah, there you are, dear. I must say I was very disappointed you couldn't see fit to collect my dress. You knew I expected you to bring it home. Now then, where have you been? *And with whom*?' She leaned back in her chair awaiting a full explanation.

Delcie could see no reason for evading the truth. She'd tell them exactly what happened, she decided—or at least part of it. 'Actually I was on my way to collect the dress,' she began, then went on to explain the circumstances of the collision. 'His hand was badly hurt,' she finished.

Aunt Alice was sympathetic. 'Oh dear, oh dear, the poor man.'

But Aunt Lois wasn't satisfied. 'Well, you took him to the hospital. Surely that was sufficient. Why was it necessary to eat with the fellow?'

'Because—because he needed my help. Somebody had to—to cut his meat,' she added weakly and without looking at her aunt.

'That's utter rubbish,' Lois snapped. 'He could've ordered stew, or fish.' Her back straightened as she sent Delcie a hard penetrating glare. 'Did you make further arrangements to see this person? You appear to have been with him for hours.'

She shook her head. 'No, he doesn't live in Wellington. That's why he's staying at the Town House.' She hesitated before admitting, 'As it happens, he comes from near Masterton.'

The rapid glance that flashed between the aunts was not lost on Delcie, nor was she unaware of the reason for it. Her father had come from the Wairarapa district; he had owned a farm near Carterton, the neighbouring town to Masterton. 'That fellow' as the aunts referred to him, had taken her mother there.

'This man, he is a farmer?' Lois asked without appearing to sound too interested.

'Yes, although his farm is managed for him while he's writing a book about dogs.'

Lois snorted. '*Dogs*! Good gracious! Can't he find a more interesting subject than dogs?' Her tone had become scathing.

'Some people like dogs,' Alice reminded her sister. 'There's one next door.'

'*Don't* remind me of that little mongrel,' Lois almost shrieked. 'And just let it show its nose through the fence again——'

'Be fair Aunt,' Delcie was forced to protest. 'He's a well-bred corgi, a most intelligent little animal.'

'I don't care how well bred it is,' Lois declared vehemently. 'If I find it desecrating our front path again——' She turned pale, indignant eyes upon her sister. 'You remember, Alice?'

Alice nodded gravely. 'I do, indeed. It was just after you'd swept the path.'

Delcie began to laugh as she recalled the scene. It had been a Saturday morning, and there had been Aunt Lois with the straw broom going swish-swish from left to right, and there had been the corgi squatting right where she'd swept. 'It was his potty time,' she giggled. 'He needed a nice clean place. Now that's what I call really intelligent.' Her mirth grew until tears rolled down her cheeks.

Lois looked at her suspiciously. 'Control yourself, Delcie. One would almost imagine you've been drinking.'

She was unable to resist the admission. 'Yes, Aunt, I have. It was gin.' The sight of her Aunt's horror made her howl with laughter.

'You're drunk,' Lois shrilled. 'How dare you come home in this state. Go to bed at once, girl.' She turned to her sister. 'Come along, Alice, it's time we went to our own beds. There's plenty to be done in the next few days before we leave.'

Delcie wiped her eyes. 'Have you decided where we're going?'

'Down south, of course,' Lois stated firmly. 'Alice has at last seen the wisdom of Queenstown in the summer, rather than enduring the heat of Northland.' She paused in the doorway to regard Delcie, her eyes narrowing slightly. 'I must say that the incident with that man has made you look really worn out. You'd be wise to get him right out of your head. Do you understand?'

'Yes, Aunt.' The words came meekly. She knew it was an order but it was one she was unable to keep because when she lay between the sheets Brad Bellamy's face hovered before her mind.

Was he able to sleep, or was he being kept awake by the pain in his hand? It was a pity she'd never see him again because, strangely, she felt drawn towards him. But obviously, despite the kisses, he was not interested in seeing more of her, otherwise he'd have said something about it, wouldn't he? But he had failed to do so. Goodbye, Miss Linden, was all he'd said. *Goodbye.*

Why had he kissed her? she wondered. Had he felt an urge to do so, or had it been an attempt to annoy her? Had it been punishment for what she had done to him, and for the inconvenience he now had looming before him? A prim and proper miss, he considered her to be, and no doubt a budding replica of her aunts.

The thought made her cringe into the pillow, although she knew she was unlike either of them. She was like her mother, Denise, who had escaped when she found the man she loved. Aunt Alice had told her a little about her mother's appearance, she recalled.

'You're growing very like her, dear,' she had said wistfully. 'You've got her sweet generous mouth and her lovely blonde hair with its slight wave and turned-up ends. But you've got your father's dark blue eyes. Most unusual, they were——'

'We won't discuss *that fellow*,' Aunt Lois had interrupted.

Poor Aunt Lois, Delcie thought as she lay in the darkness. For years she's been boiled up with hatred. And poor Mother. Her happiness had been so short-lived. Tears for the parents she could not remember fell and soaked into the pillow until she slept.

But it was a restless sleep, filled with troublesome dreams. In some strange way she seemed to be going down a long stairway until suddenly she stopped, turned, and tried to ascend. Her feet kept moving without making any progress. At the top she could see a bright light shining on green hills, and although Brad Bellamy was away in the distance he disappeared before she could call to him.

She woke at last with the morning sun streaming across the bed and the dream still fresh in her memory. And as she recalled Brad disappearing from sight she thought, well, that figures—he said goodbye, didn't he?

The depression of the previous night returned to wrap itself about her, and, resigned to her fate, she decided to sort out a few clothes to be taken to the South Island. It was impossible to conjure up any enthusiasm for the task, but at least it would keep her mind occupied and away from Brad Bellamy. Right, get cracking, she told herself as she sprang from the bed.

A hot shower did much to soothe her irritation and she then put on a blue blouse and a pair of smart denim jeans that had been cut from a jodhpur pattern. She knew that Aunt Lois held an intense dislike for jeans, no matter how well cut, but this morning Delcie felt in a restless and rebellious mood.

When breakfast was over she dragged a suitcase from a cupboard and carried it to her room. Underclothes were flung into it first, and then she began to look at her dresses. Should she take a party dress? Huh! A fat chance she'd have of wearing it. Nevertheless she folded a peacock blue garment with full skirt, a breast-moulding bodice and a deep neckline that revealed cleavage. Aunt Lois had declared it to be indecent.

She was still considering her dresses when the ring of the front doorbell pealed through the house. Somebody collecting for charity, she thought. They always come on Saturday morning. But the next minute Aunt Alice almost ran into the room.

'There's a man to see you,' she whispered, her eyes giving little nervous blinks. 'I think it's *him*.'

Delcie's jaw dropped slightly. 'Oh, no, it couldn't be. He's gone—he said goodbye,' she muttered as she brushed past Alice and went towards the front door.

But it was, and although she expected to see the plaster on his hand it did not fail to jar her nerves. 'How is it?' she asked, her eyes riveted on the white bulge poking from the sling.

'Let's not talk about it. Let's talk about you instead.'

'How did you find me?'

'You left your address. I'm to send the doctor's bill, remember? A taxi brought me here but I've dismissed it.'

She became aware of the aunts hovering in the hall behind her. 'This is Mr Bellamy—my aunts, Miss Lois and Miss Alice Truscott.'

He gave a slightly mocking bow as he said, 'I feel as though I've met them already.'

Lois scrutinised him with a long cool stare before she said, 'You'd better come into the lounge, Mr Bellamy. Our niece has told us about your accident. Most unfortunate that you bumped into her.'

The dark brows rose. 'She said that *I* bumped into *her*?'

Alice began to twitter. 'No, no, she did not. I'm sure she said it was the other way round——'

'Be quiet, Alice.' Lois silenced her sister. 'I'm sure that, whatever the case, Mr Bellamy was not looking where he was going.'

Brad spoke crisply. 'The question, Miss Truscott, lies in where I'm going now. I've been inconvenienced to the extent of being put into a most awkward position. I have a publisher's contract with a deadline to be fulfilled, and as your niece caused this damnable situation I've come to ask for her assistance.'

Lois's eyes glittered. 'I don't understand you, Mr Bellamy. My niece did her best by taking you to the hospital——'

'Where they put my hand in plaster, as you can see.'

'Yes, well, it was necessary, I suppose,' Lois retorted.

'How do you imagine I can type with it? We're talking about a book manuscript, Miss Truscott, not just a few notes or letters.'

'Surely you'll find help somewhere?' Lois's tone was defiant.

'I intend to do so. That's why I'm here. Your niece told me she teaches typing in a commercial college.'

'Yes, yes she does,' Alice put in eagerly. 'But they've now closed for the end of the year. They won't open again until about February or March——'

'Quiet, Alice,' snapped Lois furiously. 'I don't know what this man's remarks are leading up to, but I'm not sure I like what I think he has in mind.'

Delcie decided it was time she joined in this discussion which so obviously concerned herself. She crossed the room and as she stood before him she looked up into his face. 'What exactly have you in mind, Mr Bellamy?' she asked quietly.

The brown eyes looked into her own. 'It's simple enough. I want you to come home with me, to help me finish the manuscript. There's much typing to be done.'

She could hardly believe her ears. 'You mean, to Bellairs?'

'But that's ridiculous,' Lois said coldly.

Brad turned to face her. 'Why is it ridiculous, Miss Truscott?'

'Because Delcie is coming away with us, Mr Bellamy,' Lois declared firmly. 'We're leaving for the South Island in a few days.'

'Has she no say in this matter? Is she unable to speak for herself?' His words held a sting.

'Of course she's able to speak for herself,' Lois snapped back at him. 'She'll tell you where her duty lies.'

'What you're saying is that she's unable to please herself,' he drawled.

'Nothing of the sort.' Lois drew herself up to her full height. 'Young man, I'll have you know that Delcie has been reared to do the right thing. She owes it to us, Mr Bellamy, and that's all there is to be said about it.'

Alice began a hesitant suggestion. 'Lois, dear, don't you think Delcie should be allowed to say what she'd like to do? I feel it's the only way to convince Mr Bellamy that she'd prefer to—to accompany her aunts.'

'A very good idea. Let's put it to the test,' Brad snapped as he glared down into Delcie's upturned face. His eyes were full of mockery and there was a sardonic twist to his mouth. 'Well, do you know what you want to do?' he demanded aggressively.

She nodded helplessly and in silence, her eyes giving him the message but her tongue being unable to find the words. She knew that her two aunts waited for her to say she'd be going with them, but the words that eventually came were inane. 'They'd be so very disappointed,' she whispered.

'And what about me?' he gritted. 'You know the situation I'm in, the mess you've put me in. You said you'd do anything to help me. *Anything*—remember? So much for your word,' he sneered. 'It's not worth the squeak of a mouse.'

She felt appalled by his scorn, at the same time recalling that she had promised to help.

Lois took advantage of her continued silence. 'There, you see?' she said with satisfaction.

Brad swung round to face her, his voice snarling with anger. 'As for you, Miss Truscott, I consider both you and your sister to be strapping women who can fend for yourselves. If you were honest you'd admit you don't really need Delcie to go with you, but you like to think you've got little Cinderella under your thumb. Isn't that the situation?'

Lois turned crimson with anger. 'How dare you? *How dare you*?' she hooted furiously.

But he shouted her down. 'You gabble and yammer about what she owes you. What about the freedom of choice you owe her? She's got her own life to live, or do you expect her to spend it waiting on you hand and foot?'

Alice was aghast. 'Did Delcie tell you these things about us?'

'No, she did not, but the fact that you expect her to spend her holiday season with you speaks for itself.' He turned again to Delcie, his attitude one of supressed impatience. 'Now then, either you pack a bag and come with me, or you crawl under their skirts and stay there. And don't forget that coming with me means we'll be staying in motels during research. I mean together and alone,' he added in loud clear tones.

Alice sank into a chair. 'Staying in motels—— Oh, dear, oh, dear! Really, I feel quite faint.'

But Lois was made of sterner stuff. She strode closer to Brad, glaring at him as she demanded shrilly, 'Are you blatantly admitting you intend to compromise our niece?'

'We must move with the times,' he retorted nonchalantly. 'But don't worry, your niece need have no fear of rape.'

'*Rape*! Oh, dear . . .' Alice echoed weakly.

Lois pointed a quivering finger towards the door. '*Get out*!' she shouted furiously. 'Get out of this house at once—*at once*—do you hear me?'

'I hear you, Miss Truscott, and so, probably, do the neighbours.' He turned to Delcie. 'I'll give you three minutes in which to make up your mind. The Wairarapa railcar leaves in a little over an hour.'

Delcie took a deep breath, realising that her decision had already been made. Brad was right when he had declared that the aunts could fend for themselves, but she knew it pleased them to have her at their beck and call, attending to their travel arrangements. They expected her to carry their luggage, and it suited them nicely to ride in her car rather than go by public transport.

'Well?' he demanded, looking as if he could gladly shake her.

'Yes, I'll come with you,' she said in a firm and defiant tone.

CHAPTER THREE

THE cries of dismay that echoed from the aunts were a mixture of 'Oh, dear' and 'How can you do this to us?' until Aunt Lois's voice took over.

'This is history repeating itself,' she boomed. 'If your poor mother hadn't gone with that—*that fellow*, she'd be alive today. And to think that you, after all the warnings we've given you, would go into that Wairarapa district of all places with a man you've only just met—a complete stranger. Disgusting, that's what it is—utterly *disgusting*.'

Delcie did not stop to listen, nor was it necessary because the tirade from Aunt Lois followed her into the bedroom where she began throwing more articles of clothing into the open suitcase. It was strange that she should have been packing it when he arrived, she thought. Did this mean she was fated to return to the Wairarapa? Had destiny been the cause of that meeting on the stairway?

Her thoughts in a whirl, she tossed further items such as shoes and toiletries into the case until suddenly she became calm. After all, she was going for only a short time—not for ever as the stuffed suitcase seemed to indicate.

At last she flung on a blue denim jacket that matched the jodhpur-like jeans and carried the case into the lounge where the aunts stared at her in stony silence. 'I'm sorry,' she said to them. 'Please do try to understand that this is something I have to do. I promised to help in any way I could, and I must keep that promise.' She looked at them appealingly.

Aunt Alice stepped forward and kissed her. 'I think I

know how you feel, dear,' she said with a nervous glance at her sister.

But Lois merely glared at Delcie as she prepared a last salvo. 'You know what this means, of course? It's the end of this year's holiday for Alice and myself. We wouldn't dream of going without you. Now we'll have to stay home.'

'I'm sorry, Aunt,' Delcie said, her face pathetic.

Brad Bellamy looked at her with satisfaction. 'Good girl. Now then, about transport—who owns that Honda Civic?'

'It's my car,' she informed him.

'Do you wish to use it, or go by railcar?'

'She'll go in her own car,' Lois broke in furiously. 'She can then return home at a moment's notice—if she happens to come to her senses,' she added bitterly.

Brad picked up Delcie's case and carried it out to the car, then directed her to drive to the Town House where his own luggage waited to be collected. He also insisted upon ordering coffee and sandwiches before they left, and as Delcie sipped the hot drink she felt as though everything was as unreal as the stairway in last night's dream.

A short time later they were making their way out of Wellington and along the thickly built-up area of the Hutt Valley. Beyond it the highway wound over hills towards the Rimutaka Range, and as Delcie negotiated the curving mountain road the man beside her sat in silence until they were nearing the top.

'Stop at the summit,' he requested.

She did so, pulling to a parking area on the roadside. Below them and stretching away into the distance lay a wide valley of fertile land.

'There it is, the Wairarapa Valley,' he said. 'For some reason your aunt appears to have taken a real dislike to it, and I can't help wondering why.'

'It's because my mother went to the Wairarapa when she married my father.' She hesitated, then told him about her aunt's antagonism towards her mother's marriage.

'Tell me about your father.'

She put the car into gear and as it glided round the downhill twists and turns she said, 'I know so little about him. He came out from England as a young man because he wanted to learn farming. After he'd been here a few years his only relative in England died and left him a legacy. He then bought a property and married my mother. They'd been married only four years, and I was three, when they were both killed in a car accident.'

'What happened to the property?'

'It was sold and the money was invested for me.'

'Ah, I see it all—the aunts depend on you for financial help. No doubt they want to keep you pinned down.'

She rose to their defence. 'That's not exactly true,' she protested. 'Naturally I pay my way, but the aunts are not really poverty-stricken——'

'It's just that they prefer spending your money to their own,' he added ironically. 'Aunt Lois must have made your life a misery.'

'Not all the time,' she defended loyally. 'I can remember happy days when they took me to one of the beaches or to a park which had swings. You see, they hardly knew what to do with a little girl. Later they sent me to an expensive boarding school, and then to the commercial college where I learnt to do something useful——'

'Like typing the odd manuscript which might come to light,' he suggested grimly. 'Naturally your own inheritance money paid for all this education?'

'Naturally. What else would you expect? Aunt Lois had control of the finance.'

'I'll bet she did,' he snorted.

'When I was young Aunt Alice read stories to me, but if I fell over it was always Aunt Lois who bandaged skinned elbows.'

'While Aunt Alice fluttered helplessly? Which reminds me, I've neglected to ask after your poor skinned knees.'

'They're all right,' she said briefly, then added, 'Incidentally, Mr Bellamy, your constant little reminders of my part in your misfortune are becoming a bore. If they continue I shall have no option but to go home at once. Is that understood?'

'Point taken, Miss Linden. I suppose it's useless trying to convince you that the question arose from genuine concern for yourself. Or is that too much for you to believe?'

'Yes, Mr Bellamy, I'm afraid it is.'

After that there was silence while Delcie concentrated on the road which, having left the Rimutaka hill, continued towards the small settlements of Featherston, Greytown and Carterton. Beyond the latter lay the larger town of Masterton, and here the long main street was lined by shops on either side.

Delcie was directed to drive straight through and then turn right; the road then took an easterly direction through undulating country. After a few miles a tree-sheltered entrance which gave access to an avenue of tall poplars was indicated. She turned into it, and as the car reached the garden area she was given a view of a solidly built two-storeyed house. It had a brick base, white stucco walls and dark battens reaching up into high gables.

She stopped the car near the steps leading up to the front verandah, and then became aware of the woman who crossed the lawn towards them. Her dark hair had wings of grey at the temples, and her slim height seemed to stamp her as Brad Bellamy's mother. She carried an oval flower basket of long-stemmed rosebuds and, while she sent a glance of curiosity towards Delcie, a cry of dismay escaped her as her hazel eyes rested upon her son's plaster-covered hand. 'Brad, my dear, what on earth has happened?'

'Oh, just a bit of an accident.' He brushed the subject aside as he introduced Delcie. 'Mother, this is Miss Linden. I've engaged her as my typist.'

The words surprised Delcie. She had no recollection of any definite engagement as his typist. However, she smiled inwardly and let it pass as she got out of the car and shook hands.

'Well, it looks as if you'll be staying with us,' Joan Bellamy said, a small worried frown appearing between her dark brows. 'We'd better go inside and get you settled. Can you carry her case, Brad? The middle room upstairs, I think.'

They entered the wide front hall. A staircase rose from near the end of it, and at the top was a landing which gave access to several bedrooms and two bathrooms. Thick wall-to-wall carpets covered the floors and the furnishings, Delcie noticed, were modern.

'We'll put you in here,' Joan Bellamy said, leading her into a room with views over the countryside. 'Get yourself settled and then come downstairs for a cup of tea. The bathroom is across the passage. I'll find towels——'

'Thank you,' Delcie murmured, wondering if she had detected an aloof coolness in Mrs Bellamy's voice, or had this been her imagination?

Brad placed her suitcase on a stand meant for the purpose, and as he followed his mother from the room his words returned to her mind. *Engaged as his typist?* Did this mean he thought he was employing her? The situation as she saw it was to give him assistance, this being a sort of retribution on her part for having caused the accident which had put him out of action as far as typing was concerned. She had no thought of being compensated for her services, nor did she expect him to offer her a salary. If he did she would refuse to accept it, she told herself firmly. It was the only way in which she could feel better about the whole unfortunate affair.

She did not completely unpack her case, deciding to finish it later, and when she went downstairs her feet made no sound in the hall. As she stood hesitating and wondering which way to go, Joan Bellamy's voice came to her ears, agitation in it ringing clearly. 'Exactly who is this girl, Brad?'

'Delcie Linden. Didn't you catch her name?'

'Why did you bring her here? You know perfectly well that Mandy is capable of doing any typing you wish to have done.'

'This girl is an expert, Mother. Amanda is not.'

'All Mandy needs is a little practice.'

'This girl *teaches* typing, Mother. She'll have speed and efficiency. I don't want the second half of the manuscript to be botched by a mass of corrections. I've seen Amanda's typing efforts. They're not the best,' Brad argued.

'You could have hired a public typist from Masterton.'

'Yes, I did think of it.'

'Then, why bring her here?'

'So that I can work in conjunction with her. A public typist would be doing the job miles away and at times there could be discussions about alterations.'

'Does she mean anything to you, this girl?' The question was snapped at Brad abruptly.

He laughed. 'Of course not.'

'Then that's all right. I'm sure you're well aware of my dearest wish as far as Mandy is concerned.'

'Only an idiot could miss your continuous hints, Mother.'

Delcie felt a surge of panic. It would be ghastly if somebody came into the hall and found her eavesdropping. She moved towards the open front door and stood gazing across the garden without seeing any of it while one fact hammered in her mind. She was an unwelcome guest in this house. Brad Bellamy's mother did not want her to be here.

She was startled when he spoke from behind her. 'I was beginning to wonder if you were lost.'

She turned to face him, her blue eyes wide yet shadowed with apprehension. 'I'm sure your mother would prefer it,' she said.

The dark brows drew together. 'What do you mean?'

Delcie hesitated, then decided to be honest. 'I came downstairs a short time ago,' she admitted. 'What I overheard clearly indicated she'd prefer me to—get lost. I think the sooner this job is done, the happier she'll be.'

He sent her a penetrating stare. 'Did she upset you?'

'Perhaps disturbed would be a better word. You've already told me of her hopes concerning you and Amanda, so I can understand her feelings at the sight of your arrival home with—with somebody else.'

He gave a short laugh. 'Don't let it worry you. Come and have a cup of tea.'

He led her into the living-room where his mother sat in a sunny window-seat. Beside her was a trolley bearing a silver teapot, fine bone china cups and saucers and a plate of homemade cakes.

'Come and sit beside me,' Joan Bellamy invited, offering a first faint hint of friendliness. 'Do you take milk?'

As she poured the tea, a girl of about seventeen came into the room. She sent a quick shy glance towards Brad, then one of curiosity towards Delcie as she said, 'Excuse me, Mrs Bellamy, Mum wants to know if Amanda—I mean if Miss Stafford will be here for dinner tonight.'

'Yes, of course she'll be here. I've already phoned to invite her.' Joan smiled with a rapid side glance towards Brad. 'And Sally, this is Miss Linden, who'll be staying with us for a—a short time. Please tell your mother there'll be four of us at the dinner table.'

'Very well, Mrs Bellamy.' Sally's grey eyes sent Delcie a long stare of undisguised interest before she left the room.

'Sally's mother is our housekeeper,' Joan explained to Delcie. 'Olga Brown has been here for years, and we've given Sally the job of being our housemaid. It won't satisfy her for ever, but in the meantime she's happy while she has a horse at her disposal.' She turned to Brad. 'Now then, dear, you haven't told me what happened to your hand.'

He brushed the subject aside. 'Oh, I just slipped and fell.'

'But how, and where, for heaven's sake?'

Delcie felt she must admit the truth. She opened her mouth to speak but he silenced her with a warning glare as he stood up and spoke impatiently. 'If you've finished your tea I'll show you where you'll be working.'

'My goodness, we are bossy,' his mother remarked.

Delcie followed him meekly, being well aware that his tone had indicated that the situation between them was to be kept to a strictly employer-employee relationship. Granted, he had kissed her, but that was now in the past when he had thought they wouldn't be meeting again. He had said a very definite goodbye, she recalled.

His mother spoke as they reached the doorway. 'Amanda will be here soon, Brad, so don't become too involved with work. Besides, Miss Linden will probably be tired after driving all that way from Wellington.'

Delcie turned to smile at her. 'I'm anxious to start work as soon as possible, Mrs Bellamy. And please call me Delcie. Miss Linden is thrown at me non-stop at college. It makes me feel like an elderly spinster.'

The older woman looked at her gravely. 'Anyone looking less like an elderly spinster I've yet to see. Very well, take her to your holy of holies, Brad, but don't forget Amanda.' The warning in her voice rang clearly.

He laughed. 'Who could do that, Mother?'

He led Delcie to the end of a side passage and into a room that had glass doors opening on to a side verandah. It was essentially a man's room with leather chairs and an oak desk with a filing cabinet standing beside it, while along the opposite wall was a bench which held a typewriter and a tape recorder.

Looking about her she said, 'The room appears to be divided into two areas.'

'Observant girl! The desk and filing cabinet are kept entirely for farm accounts and records, while the workbench is for literary efforts. People don't come in here unless invited.'

'Except Amanda,' she said drily.

He ignored the comment as he said, 'You'll find everything you want in these drawers beneath the bench—typing and carbon paper, new typewriter ribbons.'

She raised her eyes to the bookshelf above the bench. Most of the volumes on it were reference books concerned with various aspects of New Zealand history, but then her attention was caught by a row of books with his name on the spines. There were almost a dozen of them, the sight jolting her into a shock that made her jaw sag. *Brad Bellamy!* Of course—he was *the* Brad Bellamy and she hadn't been awake to the fact.

Staring at the books, she said contritely, 'You'll think I'm a half-witted idiot, but I didn't realise you were so well-known as an author.'

'Why not? You knew my name and that I'm working on a book.'

'You can put it down to my stupidity and the fact that I didn't give it enough thought. And there was all the upset with your hand. No wonder you were raving mad.'

'Now that I have your help I'm no longer raving mad.'

'And there was also the upset with the aunts,' she continued, trying to find more excuses for not having recognised his name as being one of note, at least in her own country.

His voice had an edge to it as he accused, 'What you're really admitting is that my name didn't mean a damned thing to you because you don't read my books. Have you ever read even one of them?' he pursued relentlessly.

She felt embarrassed but had to be honest. 'No, I'm afraid not.'

'What do you read, if anything?' His tone had become slightly scathing. 'Or do you merely watch the goggle-box?'

'After a day's work in a typing class I like to relax with romance,' she told him defiantly.

'Does that mean there's absolutely no romance in your life, so you find it in books?' he asked quietly, his hand gently touching her cheek.

'It's possible,' she agreed, unaware of the despondent note in her voice, but fully conscious that his touch had made her cheek tingle. 'Perhaps during my short stay here I'll be able to catch up on reading them all.'

'Yes, well, I'd prefer to see your attention centred on the current one. You can begin by deciphering the tapes.' He opened a drawer at the end of the bench. 'Here we have at least a dozen of them, and, as I mentioned before, they have to be listened to carefully with every word being taken down so that I can assess what to use and what to discard. He slipped a tape into the recorder, pressed a button and the voice came.

Delcie listened for only a few moments before she stopped the tape, then pressed a button to reverse it to the beginning. She rolled a piece of paper into the typewriter, settled herself before it and tapped out a few lines to accustom herself to the feel of the machine. She then set the tape recorder going again and as she listened to a voice recounting the story of a dog her fingers touched the keys at speed.

He watched the words flowing on to the page. 'By jove, you're certainly fast! I must say that's excellent.'

'Thank you,' she returned drily, aware of an inner glow as she noticed the brown eyes looking at her with something that had not previously been there. Was it a new kind of respect?

A calm voice spoke from behind them. 'May I ask what it is that is "excellent"?'

Delcie twisted in her chair to face the tall dark-haired girl who watched them from the doorway. It didn't need Brad's introduction to tell her who she was.

His voice was casual as he said, 'Hello, Mandy. Meet Delcie Linden. Delcie, this is Amanda Stafford.'

Amanda sent Delcie little more than a brief nod as she entered the room. Her voice was full of concern as she said, 'Brad—your hand. What have you done to it?'

He shrugged the question away in an offhand manner. 'Oh, it's just a couple of fingers that got in the way of a heavier weight. They'll mend sooner or later, but in the meantime they're not capable of coping with this machine, so I've brought Delcie home to help me get on with the job.'

Amanda gave an exclamation of protest. 'Did you forget that I can type?' Eyes that glowed like hot coals flashed a look of disdain at Delcie's blonde hair.

'I hadn't forgotten, Amanda,' he returned calmly, 'but I also know that, at the moment, speed is of the essence because I have only until the end of February to finish the manuscript. Do you consider yourself to be a rapid typist.'

The dark eyes widened as they gazed at him. 'You *know* I'd work day and night——'

'And the more weary you became the more typing errors there'd be. You see, it's all a matter of not letting the publisher down,' he added softly. 'The man is relying on me.'

'Blast the publisher!' she snapped with unexpected vehemence. 'Oh, yes, I know all about the routine of getting it typeset, proof-read, printed and into the shops before Christmas. I've heard it all before, but what does it matter?'

'It matters to me, Amanda. I've signed a contract which I don't intend to break.'

Her voice became brittle as she gave him a long steady look. 'I see. What you're really saying is that your contract with the publisher is more important to you than—than our——' The words faltered on her lips and, turning abruptly, she walked from the room with her head held high.

Delcie felt misgivings. 'I'm afraid you've annoyed her,' she whispered. 'She's probably very hurt.'

'She should have more consideration for my problem,' he retorted. 'She knows damned well she's a poor typist. There was a time when she thought she'd like to do office work in Masterton and she started to learn typing, but she became bored and never kept it up.'

'What a pity. She could have been a real help to you. You could have worked together, side by side.'

'Is that a fact?' he drawled. At the same time his eyes raked her features as though dissecting them one by one, and once more his left hand unexpectedly stroked her cheek.

She drew away from him, her pulses reacting to his touch. 'Do you want me to continue with the tapes?' she asked. It was an effort to keep her voice steady.

'Not at the moment. Your car is still near the front

steps. We'll find a place to garage it.'

They walked through the door to the side verandah, then followed the drive to where her Honda Civic had been left. Across the lawn they could see his mother snipping full-blown heads from roses while Amanda stood beside her. A swift glance showed Delcie that Brad's eyes had narrowed slightly as he observed them, and she guessed he suspected they were discussing him—and his association with herself.

The drive continued to encircle the house and as they drove to the back he directed her towards a long open shed which was already occupied by a smart grey Renault, a red Toyota and a yellow Austin Mini. 'The Mini belongs to Amanda,' he told her. 'I think you can squeeze in beside it.'

They returned to the house through the back door and as they entered the kitchen he introduced her to a short, plump woman whose grey eyes smiled from a pleasant face. 'This is Olga Brown.'

Delcie stepped forward, her hand outstretched. 'I can see you're Sally's mother,' she smiled, 'but you look more like her sister.'

Olga Brown beamed. She wasn't used to people bothering to shake hands with her, and as they left the room they heard Sally's audible whisper of, 'I told you so.'

Dinner, that evening, proved to be an embarrassing period for Delcie. The meal was eaten in the dining-room, but with very little bright chatter to lift the tense atmosphere at the mahogany table. Instead of being relaxed, the conversation between the courses of roast beef and apple pie was positively stilted until Joan Bellamy turned to her son with an air of determination.

'Now then, Brad, I demand to know exactly what happened to your hand. I know you've been evading the subject——'

'Forget it, Mother,' he said tersely. 'It was only a bit of a collision.'

Her face had a taut expression. 'I shall not forget it. I want to know what happened. It was a collision with what?'

'I said to forget it, Mother,' he scowled.

Delcie turned to him beseechingly. 'Why don't you tell them? They might as well know what happened.' Then, coming to a decision she added, 'If you don't tell them, I shall.'

Joan Bellamy leaned forward to look at Delcie. 'You know what happened to Brad's hand?'

'Only too well. I was there.'

Brad's brows rose. 'You really want them to know?'

'Yes. Otherwise it'll be like bearing a guilty secret the whole time I'm in this house.'

'They'll have your guts for garters,' he warned.

She sent him a faint smile. 'So what? I'm used to awkward situations. You're forgetting Aunt Lois.'

'Good at garters, is she?'

'An expert.' Delcie turned to face Joan Bellamy and, ignoring a faint niggling apprehension, she explained, 'I'm afraid I caused Brad's accident. I bumped into him on the stairway between Lambton Quay and The Terrace. We fell down together and my knee crashed down on his hand, my whole weight behind it.'

'I don't believe you.' The flat statement came from Amanda.

'You don't?' Delcie's eyes widened with surprise as she turned to her. 'Why, may I ask?' she demanded quietly.

'I mean I don't believe it was an accident.' Amanda's voice was studied and cold.

Delcie was almost at a loss for words until she managed to ask, 'Are you saying you believe I bumped into him deliberately?'

'That's right. That's what I believe.'

'But why would I do that?'

'Because of who he is, of course. He's a well-known author. You saw him coming, you recognised him at once and deliberately bumped into him so that you could strike up an acquaintance.'

Brad laughed. 'Mandy, your imagination does you credit.'

She turned upon him. 'Can't you see it for yourself? She's a little go-getter.'

'How dare you?' Delcie snapped, her face pale with anger. 'You know nothing of the circumstances—there was a howling gale blowing, I had dust in my eyes——'

'But not enough to stop you from seeing who was coming,' Amanda sneered mockingly.

Brad came to Delcie's defence sufficiently to snarl, 'You'll mind your tongue, Amanda.'

His mother snapped an interruption. 'Please stop this bickering. So your collision occurred on the stairway, Brad. What happened then? Did you go to a doctor?'

'Delcie drove me to the hospital where it received attention. When she knew I'd be unable to type she offered to help. That's all there is to it.'

There was no mention of dinner at the Town House, Delcie noticed as she added to his explanation. 'He told me he was writing a book, but I didn't realise who he was until I saw that row of published works in the office. After all, lots of people try to write books——'

'Poof—a likely story,' Amanda cut in with another sneer. 'Didn't he tell you his name?'

'Yes, but I didn't connect it with the writer who's so well-known,' Delcie admitted.

'Well known? You silly little twit, he's *famous!*' Amanda's tone became even more scathing as she gave a derisive laugh. 'You expect us to believe you didn't know who to bump into when the opportunity presented itself? You must think we're dim-witted.'

Delcie felt shaken by this verbal warfare. Although she'd suffered attacks from Aunt Lois, this was something entirely different. It was not that she really cared about suspicions held by Amanda or Mrs Bellamy; the burning question was, what did Brad himself think?

Had the seeds sown by Amanda taken root in his mind? Did he now believe she had deliberately bumped into him? Turning to face him she was appalled by the frown of doubt ridged between his brows, and by the questions lurking within the brown eyes as they regarded her. His silence, too, disturbed her.

'Well, Mr Bellamy,' she demanded, her chin held slightly higher than usual. 'What do you believe? Just give me the slightest hint that you believe Amanda's deductions and I'll be out of this house so fast you'll wonder if I've ever been in it.'

He sent her a penetrating glare. 'You'll go back on your word to help me?'

'I sure will—and without a moment's hesitation. I don't hang round a man who imagines I've bent over backwards to get to know him. He can go hopping sideways.' Pride, coupled with a rising temper, caused her to tremble.

'I believe you mean it,' he drawled.

'You can say that again!' The scene on the stairway flashed into her mind and her voice became accusing. 'Don't forget, Mr Bellamy, it takes two to make a collision. You could've watched your own steps a little more carefully.'

'That's true,' he admitted, watching her narrowly. 'So what will you do?'

Joan cut in before Delcie could answer. 'She'll stay and help you, of course. Anyone with less than half an eye can see she's not the type of person who would let you down, especially after she's given her word.'

Brad gave a short laugh. 'Thank you for trying,

Mother, but I doubt that she's the type to be fooled by flattery.'

'Nor am I the type of person who'll remain in a place where I'm likely to be insulted,' Delcie informed them with a cold glance at the dark-haired girl sitting opposite her.

'So?' Brad put the the question patiently while Joan watched her with anxious eyes.

She considered the question carefully, and as she recalled the overheard conversation between Brad and his mother she realised that Joan Bellamy did not want her to be here. In short she was unwelcome, and this unhappy feeling was reflected in the troubled depths of her eyes as she turned to Joan.

'I'll leave first thing in the morning. Amanda can take over the typing. She won't work as quickly as I would, but she'll get the job done eventually.'

'What about my time limit?' Brad asked with an edge to his voice.

She turned to him, her eyes still troubled. 'I'm afraid you'll just have to let the publisher know the manuscript will be late through circumstances beyond your control. They'll undertand.'

He stared at her in silence, and as she waited for his comment she noticed a glance of veiled triumph shoot from Amanda to Joan. It irritated her to the extent of making her feel she could no longer stay in the room, so she stood up and prepared to leave the table. 'If you'll excuse me, Mrs Bellamy, I'll go back to the office and do more work on the tapes.'

Brad said, 'I'll be grateful for that much at least.' He paused before adding casually, 'Actually I intended taking you to Otaki tomorrow. There's an elderly couple I wish to interview.'

Amanda's eyes widened. 'Otaki? That's miles across the ranges on the other coast.'

'That's right,' he told her gravely. 'There's a good motel there, and we'd have found time for a walk on the beach.'

Her face became stony. 'Are you saying you intended staying alone in a motel with this—this girl?' Amanda almost spat the words, then controlled her anger and turned to Joan. 'Or perhaps you were to go to Otaki with them?'

'No, it's the first I've heard of it,' Joan admitted faintly. She looked at Delcie with a hint of doubt in her eyes.

Delcie caught the look. 'Mrs Bellamy, I was warned there'd be interviews and trips of this sort to be made, but please don't worry—I have absolutely no intention of going to bed with your son,' she stated, then left the room with all the dignity she could muster.

CHAPTER FOUR

AFTER the dining-room's stormy atmosphere, the silence of the office seemed like a haven of peace. The sun had only recently set behind the long Tararua mountain range, and beyond them, almost in a straight line to the west, lay Otaki. It would have been pleasant to walk on the beach with Brad, she thought wistfully, but instead of dwelling on the subject she put her mind to the work of transferring the taped stories on to paper.

However, she hadn't been working long before Amanda surprised her by coming into the room, and, glancing up, Delcie noticed that the dark eyes watched her flying fingers with a hint of envy. Why had she come? she wondered, but, determined not to reveal curiosity, she ignored Amanda's presence by continuing to type.

Amanda refused to be ignored. A quick jab silenced the tape recorder as she said belligerently, 'Now you listen to me, Delcie Linden. It's only right that you understand the situation. Brad and I are going to be married. It's a long-standing arrangement that's best for all concerned.'

Delcie looked at her ringless left hand. 'Are you telling me you're offically engaged?'

'Not yet, but that's beside the point. Brad's mother desires it, my parents are keen for it, and I've set my heart on it. It means that the property will eventually return to being as it was when his grandfather bought it.'

'It sounds very clinical,' Delcie pointed out. 'It's what I call cold and calculated. Doesn't love come into it at all?'

'Of course it does,' Amanda snapped. 'I'm crazy about him.'

'But even more crazy about owning Bellairs as it used to be?'

Amanda glared at her, anger glinting from her dark eyes. 'All you have to do is pack your bags and be on your way first thing in the morning as promised. I don't want to hear of any change of mind, so don't start thinking up excuses for not leaving.'

Delcie yawned. 'Really, Amanda, I can't understand why my presence concerns you. I mean, if, as you say, your marriage arrangements are more or less all cut and dried——'

'It worries me because I can't work out why he brought you here. You must realise he could have found help nearer home. I'm also beginning to wonder exactly how long you've *really* known each other, especially as he's in the habit of making trips to Wellington.'

Delcie laughed. 'Poor Amanda. Your mind must be in a tormented whirl of doubt. Are you saying you no longer think I deliberately bumped into him?'

'I don't know what to think,' Amanda admitted.

'Well, why don't you go and sort it out with him? See, he's across the lawn beside the rosebed.' Glancing through the glass doors her eyes had caught sight of the tall figure standing in the dusk of the summer evening.

Amanda followed her gaze. 'Oh, yes, he's probably waiting for me to join him. We often walk round the roses after dinner.' She went through the door and hurried across the lawn.

Delcie sighed as she watched the tall girl take Brad's arm, and despite the fading light she knew that dark eyes were gazing up into his face. They made a handsome couple, she mused with a strange twist within her own heart, and no doubt the time would come when Brad would wake up to the fact that he loved Amanda. She sighed again and switched on the tape recorder.

The next interruption came about fifteen minutes later when Joan walked into the room and stood watching for several moments before Delcie realised she was there. The tape recorder was then again switched off as she turned to face the older woman.

'Did you wish to talk to me?' she asked politely.

Joan shook her head. 'Not really. It was just that I wondered if you'd like coffee. You left the table before we'd had it. I could bring you a cup,' she offered.

'Please don't bother' Delcie assured her.

'You know, I've never seen anyone type so rapidly. It makes me realise how—how pathetic Amanda's efforts are beside your own. I wish she'd really practice so that she could help Brad.'

'And there speaks a mother,' Delcie smiled.

'Yes, I suppose I'm wrapped up in him, but you must understand he's all I've got. You have brothers and sisters?'

'No, I'm really an orphan.' She told Joan a little about her aunts, and then she found herself recounting the story of her mother's runaway marriage, and how she'd lost her parents. 'Their place was somewhere out of Carterton,' she finished.

'Carterton isn't many miles from here,' Joan reminded her. 'I suppose you've seen where your parents lived?'

Delcie shook her head. 'I've never had the opportunity to search for it, mainly because I've had my own car for only a year.' She did not add that Aunt Lois had strictly forbidden her to go searching for skeletons.

Joan had become thoughtful. 'Linden—*Linden*——' she murmured as though raking the depths of her memory. 'I've a vague feeling I've heard that name. Did they live out towards the ranges?'

'I've no idea, except that I know there were hills. After all, it is twenty years ago.'

Joan was still deep in thought until something struck a chord. 'The Dillons—friends I haven't seen for ages—had neighbours who died in a car accident. It was years ago. They bought the property for their son. We could make enquiries if you'd consent to stay and help Brad.'

It was a bribe and Delcie knew it. She shook her head. 'I doubt that it would be the same place.'

'If it isn't I'm sure it can be traced,' Joan persisted. 'There's sure to be someone who remembers them.'

'I'll make the effort at some other time,' Delcie said in a quietly determined voice, at the same time vowing to herself that this was an assignment she would keep. Despite Aunt Lois's displeasure, she would have a weekend at Carterton and make enquiries from there.

Why hadn't she done it before? she wondered, then realised that since she'd owned her car the weekends had been dominated by her two aunts. But suddenly that state of affairs seemed to have vanished into the past, and for the first time in her life—albeit with Brad Bellamy's assistance—she had actually defied Aunt Lois. She took a deep breath as the knowledge gave her a feeling of newly found freedom.

Joan watched her curiously. 'You're smiling about something,' she said. 'Can't we share it?'

Delcie was apologetic. 'The story is too long, and instead of becoming involved in it I must get on with this job. You'll understand it's for Brad.' At least she owed him something for freeing her from the bonds of Aunt Lois, she told herself as she adjusted the extending arm of the table lamp to a better angle.

Joan took the hint and left the room, and with her departure Delcie put her mind to the words flowing from the tape recorder. As her fingers tapped the keys she became fascinated by the stories the numerous dog owners recounted about their animals, some of the incidents making her laugh, others bringing tears to her eyes, but the saddest of all being the times when a faithful four-footed friend met his end.

She was deeply moved by the thought of the expressive brown eyes becoming glazed and the tail that had wagged so joyfully becoming still. It was something that could be understood only if one had owned and lost a beloved animal, she realised.

During one pause to dab at her eyes, Brad's voice spoke from behind her. 'Is it getting to you?' he asked quietly.

She swung round to face him, her eyes still blurred. 'It's sad when they die, but it's even worse when they're ill-treated by human beings. I wouldn't have believed some of these things——'

'Needless to say I'm not including anything that's too depressing. The book's aim is to give enjoyment to dog lovers, although no doubt you'll see why everything on the tapes has to be looked at so that I know what to discard.'

She looked at the length of leg stretched before him. 'How long have you been reclining in that chair?'

'Long enough to admire your skill and speed.'

She ignored the compliment by asking, 'Where's Amanda.'

'She's gone home. I don't think she's very pleased with me.'

'She'll feel better tomorrow when she knows I've departed.'

'You really intend to leave?'

Silently she thought it would have been nice to have gone to Otaki with him, but aloud she said, 'I can't help feeling it'll be better for your domestic affairs.'

'I see. Very well.' His tone had become clipped.

She waited for him to say more, to try and reason with her or persuade her to stay, even to remind her of her promise to help him finish the book, but not one pleading word did he utter. At the same time she knew she was ready to capitulate and remain, but she now felt it would be humiliating to climb down; even more disturbing was the fact that her own stubborn pride was about to cause her to be thrown back into the lap of Aunt Lois.

Brad's words cut across her thoughts. 'You're over-tired,' he told her abruptly. 'You're not thinking straight.'

She was startled by his perception. 'How would you know anything about my thoughts?'

'Your face is troubled. It's enough to tell me they've gone completely haywire. Nor is it surprising, because you've had a busy day, what with me arriving on the mat and all that upset with the aunts, the decision to be made and the drive here, topped by Amanda's attack at the table. Yes, you've had quite a day.'

'I suppose so,' she admitted wearily.

He left the armchair. 'You'll leave that work at once and come outside for a walk. It's a lovely evening.' He opened the verandah door, then took her arm to draw her outside—and he didn't release it as they crossed the lawn towards the rosebeds.

The sky was now pricked by stars and the moon had risen to throw shadows which enveloped the garden in an aura of mystery. Delcie looked about her, and admitted, 'I'd be nervous if you weren't here. There's an eeriness about trees at night.'

His left arm went about her, drawing her closer to his side. 'Don't be afraid, little girl, there are no goblins in this garden. The perfume of the roses drives them away.'

Conscious of his touch she drew in several deep breaths. 'They really are fantastic—almost intoxicating——'

'It goes to your head?' he murmured, drawing her into the shadows beneath an archway covered by a strongly perfumed red climbing rose.

She realised that both of his arms were holding her

closely, the plaster on his right hand causing no
hindrance to the embrace, and it was only then that she
noticed he had discarded the sling which had held his
hand in an upright position.

'Your hand is feeling better?' she asked, making an
effort to appear unmoved by his closeness.

'It's not too bad.' His tone was non-committal as he
bent his head and kissed her, his mouth playing with her
lips sensuously.

Her breath quickened as the blood coursed through
her veins to make her pulses jump. *This is ridiculous. I
should push him away*, she told herself vaguely, her mind
in a whirl, but somehow she lacked the power to do so.
Instead she found herself straining against him as her
arms crept up and about his neck. Her fingers found the
hair at his nape, then gently smoothed the back of his
head while his lips traced a line to her throat.

A sigh escaped him as he said in a low voice, 'History
is repeating itself.'

She failed to catch his meaning.

'The last time I kissed you we were saying goodbye.
Was it only last evening? It seems a lifetime.'

She waited, still hoping to hear the words that would
dissuade her from departure, but none appeared to be
forthcoming. Obviously his pride prevented him from
pleading with her.

He found her mouth again, his kiss growing savage as
his rising passion called for a response she found
impossible to control. 'You're still determined to leave?'
he murmured as he pressed her against the length of his
body.

It was then that she realised that these kisses were
merely his method of persuading her to stay. Also, as far
as she was concerned, they didn't mean a thing. The
knowledge had the same effect as an icy shower; she
nodded her head and whispered faintly, 'Yes, perhaps it

would be better if I leave straight after breakfast.' She looked up at him, hoping.

'OK.' His tone was terse as he released her abruptly. 'In that case I suppose you'd prefer to go inside right now.'

Disappointed to know that her deduction had been correct, Delcie turned and walked towards the house, noticing that as she did so he made no attempt to follow her. She went to bed as soon as she could reasonably excuse herself, and as she lay between the sheets she realised there was another good reason for her departure. She was beginning to like this man far too much.

She knew he was domineering and somewhat arrogant, yet there was something about him that sparked her interest, something that made her sit up and take notice. And it didn't take too much intelligence to see that before her emotions became too deeply involved she'd be wise to run while she still had the power to use her legs.

Next morning she sprang out of bed, showered quickly and threw her unpacked belongings back into the suitcase. She carried it downstairs, and as she left it in the hall she could hear voices coming from the dining-room; she was not surprised to find Amanda sitting at breakfast with Brad and his mother.

'Amanda is here to make sure you get away safely,' Brad teased with an amused glint in his eyes.

The brunette flushed. 'I am *not*,' she denied hotly. 'I was out riding before the morning becomes too hot,' she endeavoured to explain.

Joan looked at her fondly. 'It's the best time to be riding. I must say you look very attractive in jodhpurs, my dear.'

Amanda gave a faint smile, indicating that this was something she already knew.

The conversation at the table continued to be light, still with no suggestion from Brad that she should change her mind. Watching him covertly, Delcie found difficulty in keeping her eyes from his handsome face. His smart tan safari suit made her realise that even on a Sunday morning he was well dressed, and by the time he carried her suitcase out to the garage she was feeling thoroughly depressed.

The Honda Civic was parked beside the grey Renault, and, after saying a polite goodbye to Joan and Amanda, Delcie slid behind the wheel. Tears pricked behind her lids as she turned the ignition key, but vanished when there was no response. The motor was dead. She tried again, and again, but still without the slightest kick of life.

Brad said, 'I suspect your battery is flat, or perhaps it could be something more serious.' He lifted the front, peered at the motor, then slammed the bonnet shut again.

Amanda had gone slightly pale. 'You try to start it, Brad,' she pleaded almost desperately. 'Delcie's probably doing something stupid like—like flooding the motor.'

He shook his head. 'As you can see, I'm only a one-fisted mechanic. I'm afraid it's beyond me.' Then turning to Delcie he rasped, 'As you're so determined to leave this place I'll drive you in the Renault. Your car can be serviced during the week.'

'But you can't drive,' she protested. 'Perhaps I should wait——'

He silenced her by cutting in coldly, 'The Renault is an automatic. It shouldn't be too difficult.'

Further argument was strangled by the sight of her case being snatched from the Honda and dumped on the back seat of the grey car. He then opened the front passenger door and waited in silence for her to get in.

Amanda spoke eagerly. 'I'll come with you. I'll be company on the way home.'

'Not today, Amanda.' The words were snapped

bluntly as he took his place behind the wheel. Despite his injured hand, he managed the steering surprisingly well as he backed out of the garage.

Delcie sat in silent misery as they drove towards the main highway. Everything seemed to have tumbled about her ears in the form of a giant anticlimax, and the fact that he'd go to these lengths to be rid of her left her feeling thoroughly shaken. Very little was said as they drove through Masterton, and by the time the car had sped through Carterton and Greytown she was in a state of battling against breaking down to weep copious tears.

She had a grip on herself when they reached Featherstown at the bottom of the eighteen-hundred-foot Rimutaka Hill, and as they climbed over the range she had to admire his left-handed dexterity in manipulating the wheel round the twists and turns of the high mountain road. Watching him helped to divert her mind, and by the time they reached the flat Western Hutt road she had become resigned to the fact that her brief sojourn with Brad Bellamy was almost over. Tomorrow it would be like a dream.

Misery engulfed her again and she barely noticed when he changed traffic lanes to make a right-hand turn; however, when he reduced speed to negotiate a corner that took them from the main highway and on to a different road, she sat upright and exclaimed, 'You've left the Hutt Road, this isn't the way to Wellington.'

'No.' His tone became nonchalant as he grinned at her. 'But we're not going to Wellington. We're going to Otaki. Had you forgotten?'

She was speechless. Her jaw dropped slightly, and as her spirits began to soar her nervous tension vanished. At last she found words. 'You're a wretch—a cunning, wily wretch!' she accused with some force. 'You had this planned all the time.'

'Desperate situations need desperate measures, and I

had to take drastic steps to retain your services. Now admit you're glad to be coming with me.'

'Yes, I'm glad.' She didn't wish to sound too eager and she knew she must keep her feet on the ground because it was merely her *services* he needed.

He sent her a side glance. 'Then why such determination to leave the job?'

'I felt I had to get away. It was really because I was so upset over the accusations Amanda made about deliberately trying to get to know you. And when I thought you actually believed them it—it was too much. I just wanted to go home.'

He laughed softly. 'Silly goose, how could I believe such rot? Had you forgotten we collided on the bend of the stairs? You couldn't possiblly have seen who was coming up.'

'I'm afraid I was too angry to think straight. Why didn't you explain that fact to Amanda?'

'Because the whole argument was too ridiculous to be discussed. Does that make you feel happier?'

'Yes, much happier.' A smile lit her features as she took a deep breath and relaxed in the comfort of the front passenger seat, and suddenly the surrounding landscape seemed to be a brighter place until a disturbing thought struck her. 'You haven't any luggage,' she exclaimed. 'And what about the tape recorder?'

He grinned. 'They're in the boot of the car.'

She glanced at him suspiciously. 'And my car . . .?'

'It'll be OK when I replace the distributor which I removed early this morning.'

'You—you cunning devil,' she accused again, still happy with the knowledge that he wanted her to be with him, even if only for the assistance she would be able to give to him.

The road went through green undulating farmlands until it reached the main highway on the west coast of the lower North Island. It then turned north and ran through a number of small settlements until it came to the township of Otaki. A left-hand turn took them to the beach area where there were numerous holiday cottages and homes for retired people.

There was also a motel, the sight of which filled Delcie with a feeling of nervous tension, which didn't leave her as she followed him into the building's small office. She stood self-consciously while he spoke to the girl at the reception desk.

'A two-bedroom unit, please,' he demanded nonchalantly.

'Certainly, sir.' The girl looked at him with interest then flicked a quick glance in the direction of Delcie's left hand.

The register was pushed towards Brad. He signed it, then handed the pen to Delcie, his manner completely casual.

She was startled. She had not expected to sign her name, nor did she see the necessity to do so. It was just devilish teasing on his part, she suspected. However, she took the pen and as she wrote her name she was consumed by guilt born of her puritanical upbringing. Here she was, about to stay in a motel with a man she had met only the day before yesterday. Thoughts of the horror that would be expressed by the aunts slid into her mind, giving her an inane desire to giggle.

She also suspected that the desk girl was secretly amused. *Two* bedrooms, she was probably thinking, but only *one* to be used. Oh, yes, we've had people like you before today. However, no sign of such thoughts was apparent on her face as she led the way to the unit and told them that the dining-room was through there——

Apart from the two bedrooms, the unit consisted of a lounge with television and a small kitchen. Milk, tea and coffee were provided, while an electric stove enabled occupants to choose between going to the dining-room or preparing a meal for themselves.

Brad parked the car in the sheltered area outside their door. Their luggage was carried in and he then declared himself to be ready for lunch, so the unit was locked and they made their way to the dining-room. And while his attitude towards her indicated nothing more than a casual friendliness, Delcie was vitally aware of her own inner feelings. She was walking about a foot above the ground and her knees felt weak.

They were led to a table for two, and as they sat down he said, 'Mr and Mrs Mackenzie are expecting us at about two-thirty.'

She was surprised. 'They are?'

'I phoned this morning. He's a retired high country sheep farmer from the South Island. I've been assured he's full of stories about dogs, and I'd like to check on a few points about when the first sheepdogs came out from Scotland.'

'You certainly plan ahead,' she smiled.

'Of course. I have to. While we're chatting I'll rely on you to keep an eye on the tape. If it comes to an end while he's talking make sure we don't miss anything as it's being changed. Sometimes vital things like correct names can be lost. Do you understand?'

She nodded. 'I think so. It could leave a gap in the story.'

'Exactly. Be firm. Interrupt if necessary while the tape's being reversed or changed. And if his wife's in the room don't allow her to chatter because her voice will also come on to the tape. It could drown out what he says, and later it'll be the devil's own job to decipher some of his words.'

He paused while a waitress placed ham salads before them, and as Delcie cut his meat and anything else she considered needed slicing he watched with quiet amusement. 'Thank you. I always knew that sooner or later you'd be cutting my meat.'

She ignored the taunt, then changed the subject by asking a question that had been nagging at her. 'Why was it necessary for me to sign my name at the desk?'

He regarded her quizzically. 'You'd prefer to have the receptionist imagine we're posing as man and wife?'

She flushed. 'No, of course not. But—does Amanda always sign her name?'

'I've no idea. I've never been in a motel with Amanda. I've never taken her on one of these research trips.'

'Oh.' For some reason the knowledge pleased her although she dared not look at him lest this fact should be revealed in her eyes. One only has to look into Delcie's eyes, Aunt Alice was in the habit of saying. One then knows if she's telling the truth, and if she's happy or otherwise.

Later they found their way to the cosy seafront house of Hamish Mackenzie and his wife. He was an elderly man whose appearance indicated he had led an outdoor life, and despite his years in New Zealand his accent still echoed the Scottish Highlands. His wife was a small, smiling woman whose grey hair was neatly short and whose blue eyes twinkled knowingly.

The research session went surprisingly well. Hamish Mackenzie had listed headings for all the dog stories he wished to recount, and if his wife dared to open her mouth she was silenced by a frown from this Scot who had no intention of being interrupted by the woman in the house. However at three-thirty his quick glance at the clock sent her scuttling away to the kitchen and, when she returned with a tray of afternoon tea, the creamed sponge cake and dainty pikelets were featherlight.

The session lasted until five o'clock, and during it Delcie learned much about the value of sheepdogs. She realised that city people had no opportunity to observe the work and ability of these faithful animals, and that without canine assistance the farmers would be unable to control their own flocks.

As the clock struck five the old man stood up to indicate he'd had his say on the matter of dogs. 'Weel noo, it's time to wet the whistle with a wee drappie,' he stated with an air of finality. 'Ye canno' whistle when ye mouth's gone dry—and mine's awful dry with all that clacking aboot man's best friend. Aye, it is that.' He opened a bottle of Scotch and placed it on the table beside Brad. 'I'll not insult ye by addin' water,' he declared.

Delcie was offered sherry and as she sipped it she tried to chat with Mrs Mackenzie, but the small woman was of a retiring nature and had little to say. However, when they were leaving she managed to whisper in Delcie's ear, 'He's a bonny lad, is that man of yours. I'd like to see him in a kilt—aye, I would that.'

Delcie hesitated, her natural honesty making her feel she should explain Brad was not her man, and that he had Amanda waiting for him at home. But instinct warned that Mrs Mackenzie belonged to a generation which would not approve of her 'gaddin' aboot with another lassie's man'. And as for staying in a motel with a man before being wedded—that would be the last straw.

She prayed they'd escape before the question of their accommodation came up, and she was thankful when the tape recorder was placed on the back seat and they drove away from the Mackenzies' home. At the same time the thought of staying alone with Brad sent tingles of anticipation running up and down her spine.

He said, 'Are you ready for a walk on the beach?'

She drew a deep breath of sea air. 'Oh yes, more than ready.'

'Does that mean you were bored with all that doggy talk?'

'Not at all. I was fascinated. I had no idea a dog would put his heart into mustering sheep to such an extent, even to when his pads bleed on shingle slides.'

'Those are the things a sheepman remembers. Blood in every pawtrack, hearts so big and willing.'

They drove along the short stretch of seafront road, then parked and locked the car near an opening to the beach. A few minutes later they made their way barefoot between clumps of tall coastal-growing marram grass, the dry sand feeling cool and soft beneath their feet.

A fresh sea-breeze billowed the gathered skirt of Delcie's yellow and white sunfrock, and although the sun was still a fair distance from the horizon she was thankful for the matching jacket.

'You look like a little girl,' remarked Brad as she skipped over the firmer sand to paddle in ripples at the water's edge.

'That's just how I feel,' she called gaily. 'I haven't done this for years.'

'When and where was the last time?'

'It's so long ago I can't remember, but if I close my eyes I can see the aunts sitting on a rug with their knitting and a Thermos of tea in the basket.'

'And big hats?' Brad suggested. 'I'll bet they wore big hats.'

'Of course—*huge* hats to protect their complexions.'

They walked along the firm wet beach chatting amicably, and as Delcie drew in more deep breaths of the tangy sea air she felt as though all her cares had flown away, either beyond the ocean-girt horizon on their left, or over those high, bush-clad ranges away to the right.

She was also conscious of an intense happiness that almost amounted to a heady excitement which filled her with an inane desire to shout aloud and dance on the sand. And this, she knew, was because she was with Brad. At the same time she realised that this stupidity had to be controlled, because when she looked at him a vision of Amanda's face seemed to loom just beyond his shoulder.

They reached an area that was well beyond the view of the waterfront houses when a thin curl of smoke on the upper reaches of the beach caught Delcie's eye. She paused, pointing to it. 'Over there—somebody's had a fire.'

He frowned. 'We'd better check to make sure it's out. The wind could blow sparks into the dry marram grass.'

They wandered towards the blackened patch where driftwood had been burning, and as their feet sank into the softer sand Brad said, 'I think children have been here. They've had a picnic and have baked potatoes in the embers.'

She stared at the fire. 'How do you know?'

'Because they've left a couple—do you see those two round black lumps in the ashes? What's more, they intend to return.'

'How can you be so sure of that, Sherlock Holmes?'

'The driftwood piled beside that old log makes me wonder if it's been left to rekindle the fire.'

'And the old log, Sherlock?' she asked, laughing at his deductions, yet suspecting they were correct.

He examined it intently. 'That's the trunk of an old willow tree. Once upon a time it grew on a riverbank, happily leaning over the water until floods uprooted it and washed it down the river to the sea. It then floated along the coast until it was thrown up on this beach to provide a seat for people who light fires.'

He stirred the ashes with a piece of driftwood, and, sitting on the old trunk, they watched the embers glow into life. His jacket brushed her arm and she revelled in the quiet companionship, and in the surrounding silence broken only by the sound of waves tumbling on the shore.

At last he said. 'There are beaches on the coast beyond Masterton. I'll take you there one day.'

'That's if I'm still with you,' she pointed out soberly.

He turned to stare at her. 'Are you saying you still intend to leave before the job's done?'

She felt unable to meet his eyes, and, watching a wisp of smoke, she decided to be honest. 'It will really depend on Amanda. If she persists in making things too unpleasant for me I'll—I'll definitely go home.'

'You're saying you won't stand up to her?'

She shrugged. 'Why should I have to put up with that sort of hassle?'

'Well, that figures. You haven't shown much sign of standing up to your aunts—at least from what you've told me.'

'How can you say that? I defied them on Friday by coming away with you, didn't I?'

'It must've been a colossal effort.' Sarcasm made his voice bitter. 'I imagine that standing up to Amanda would be small in comparison.'

'You're forgetting there's not only Amanda,' she flashed at him, her anger rising. 'There's your mother as well. You might recall I overheard enough to tell me I'm not the most welcome of guests to be staying at Bellairs. Why don't you become engaged to Amanda and put both their minds at rest?'

'Because I have no intention of becoming engaged to Amanda—nor do I intend becoming engaged to anyone else. *Is that understood*?' His voice snapped with anger.

She was so appalled by his emphasis on the question that she shouted at him furiously. '*Really!* I trust you don't imagine I expect you to become engaged to *me*.'

It was then she saw the spider crawling on the plaster of his injured hand. It was about the size of a pea, with a small head and a red stripe running from front to rear across the centre of its dark velvety back. Her eyes dilated and a gasp of fear escaped her, but without hesitation she snatched up a piece of driftwood and dealt it a heavy blow, killing it instantly.

Brad leapt to his feet with an oath of pain. 'What the hell did you do that for? If you wanted to hurt you sure succeeded——'

'But nothing to the hurt you'd have got from the spider. It was a katipo. It was coming around from the lower side of the cast.'

He stared aghast at the remains on the plaster.

Delcie had sprung to her feet, her face pale. 'You do know about katipos, I suppose? You do know that their bite causes instant agonising pain that spreads through the body, and that it can be fatal?'

'Of course I know. We were idiots to be sitting on that old trunk, because under logs is where they're to be found.'

As they moved away she shook her skirt in sudden panic. 'I hope there isn't one on me——'

'We'd better make sure. Take it off at once.' In a flash his left hand had unzipped the back of her sundress and had slid the straps from her shoulders, leaving her almost naked except for her panties and bra. She stood with her arms crossed in a futile effort to conceal her rounded breasts while he squatted on the sand to minutely examine both sides of every fold of the gathered skirt.

The jacket was treated to the same scrutiny until at last both garments were handed back to her. 'I think they're OK,' he said casually. 'You can put them on again.'

'There could be another spider on you,' she said nervously.

'I doubt it.'

Nevertheless she insisted upon examining his clothes, and as she did so she realised that he hadn't bothered to give her own body as much as a second glance. He simply wasn't interested in her as a woman.

She'd stood almost completely naked in front of him, hadn't she? But his whole attention had been on her dress. Yes, she knew it was important for it to be free of spiders, and she appreciated his extreme care in going over every fold, but surely he could have favoured her body with a least the merest glance.

So what stronger proof did she need to show he had no interest in her whatever? This fact became even more obvious as they retraced their steps along the beach and his entire conversation was dominated by the subject of katipo spiders, funnel-web spiders, trap-door spiders and other creepy-crawly creatures.

CHAPTER FIVE

DELCIE found difficulty in keeping up with his long strides.

'The katipo is the only poisonous spider in New Zealand,' he informed her.

'Yes—I know——' she panted breathlessly.

'It's related to the Australian red-back and to the American black widow spider.'

She shuddered. 'Do we have to talk about them?'

'I'm told the bite is accompanied by profuse sweating, great difficulty in breathing, vomiting and convulsions——'

'Will you shut up!' she yelled at him. 'You'll make me dream about the wretched things,' Then, suddenly contrite, 'I'm sorry—I'm forgetting you've had a shock from being so close to one of those little horrors.'

'Your quick action saved me from being bitten. Thank you, Delcie, I'm grateful.'

She felt a glow of self-satisfaction that remained with her until they were back in the motel. However, it was short-lived because even as she showered and changed into a sleeveless dress of soft fuchsia with tie waist and knife-pleated skirt she found herself sliding downward towards a depression.

It became intensified after their evening meal when they were watching a television programme in which she had little interest, and then it grew worse as her thoughts began to concentrate upon a question spinning round in her mind. What action should she take when they returned to Bellairs? Should she go home as she had previously intended, or should she remain to finish the job of typing his manuscript?

What she really longed to do was clear enough in her

own mind because, now that she was beginning to know him better, the thought of leaving him gave her an ache somewhere deep within herself.

A slight turn of her head enabled her to observe him as he lounged in an easy chair, his long legs stretched before him. His handsome profile was shadowed in the dim light of a table lamp which threw rays against the folds of the drawn curtains, and in some intangible way his magnetism seemed to reach out and enfold her in an unseen mesh.

He turned to look at her, then said abruptly, 'You're not watching the film. Does it bore you?'

'It's rather violent. I hate violence on the screen so I—I began thinking of other things.'

A dark brow was raised towards her. 'Such as planning to rush back to Wellington the moment we get home?'

He was so near the truth she was startled into an admission. 'Well, I was wondering about it.'

'Then you can forget it.' The words held a ring of finality.

'And there's another thing——' She hesitated, then fell silent, wishing she hadn't spoken.

'Go on. Another thing—such as what?'

She hesitated again, then said, 'I can't help feeling I'm an evil force where some people are concerned.'

He gave a hearty laugh. 'You? An evil force? That's really funny. In what way, may I ask?'

'You can see what happened to you when we met on the stairs.'

'That was bad luck coupled with one of Wellington's gales.'

She shook her head dolefully. 'Look at your hand. You wouldn't have walked on the beach if I hadn't been with you.'

'Wrong. I always walk on the beach when I'm near one. I love striding along the sand and breathing in sea air. And you can look at it in this way, if I hadn't had my hand in plaster that katipo would've bitten me right smartly—or at least a few moments later if you hadn't killed it so quickly.'

'I'm thankful I saw it in time.'

'Right. So stop talking rubbish. You've no power to put a jinx on anyone.' He stood up and switched off the television, then took his seat beside her on the settee.

His left arm rested along the cushions at her back and she was immediately conscious of his nearness but gave no sign of it as she began miserably, 'When I became ill with whooping cough I brought more than a jinx upon my own parents——'

'What dammed humbug,' he snapped impatiently. 'Your father was obviously driving too fast. Bends on back country roads demand respect. Have you any idea exactly where it happened?'

'No, except that it was in hilly country out of Carterton. Your mother wonders if their place was bought by people she knows for their son. She said she'd make inquiries. I think she said their name is Dillon.'

He shot her a quick glance. 'Richard Dillon's place? It's possible. Richard and I were at school together. His father had the place managed until he was old enough to run it himself.' He sent her a sly grin. 'Richard is a most eligible bachelor. Would you like to meet him?'

Her chin rose a fraction. 'I'm not even remotely interested in Mr Dillon, but I'll admit I'd like to see the house. That's if it's the same place, of course.'

'We'll soon find out. If it is I'll phone and make arrangements to visit him next weekend—so long as you haven't rushed back to Wellington before then.'

It was her turn to laugh. 'And in the meantime I can get on with the typing. You're very cunning, Brad Bellamy. You're holding out a carrot you think I'm unable to resist.'

'Actually, I'm thinking more about you and Richard Dillon. It would be strange if——' He paused, his eyes narrowing thoughtfully.

She turned to stare at him. 'What are you talking about?'

'If you fell for each other like a pair of shot duck—now that would be strange. Delcie Dillon—it's got a nice ring to it.'

She laughed. 'Now who's talking rubbish? You're certainly two jumps ahead of yourself. I haven't even met the man, nor do I yet know if it's my old home.'

'But if it is I reckon you'll be half-way to succumbing to Richard's fatal charms.' Although the words were spoken lightly, his face was serious.

She became indignant. 'I've never heard such ridiculous rot. I couldn't possibly fall in love with a man at such short notice.'

'Stranger things have happened,' he snapped crisply. 'Have you never heard of love at first sight?'

'I've heard of it. I'm not sure that I believe in it.'

'I'm told that some people believe it's the only love. I'm told it can hit one like a bolt from the blue.'

She smiled. 'I'll dodge any bolts I see coming. In any case, aren't you forgetting Richard's side of the matter?'

He turned to regard her solemnly. 'Just gaze at him with those blue eyes and he'll pull you through his front door and into his arms as well. It's possible I'm being a fool to suggest taking you near his place.'

She looked at him in amazement. 'Oh? Why would that be?'

'Because I'd like to keep you to myself for a while.'

She tried to ignore the fact that he was leaning closer to her and that her pulses were thumping. 'Only for a while?' she asked lightly. 'I see. That'll be to get your typing done, of course.'

'Don't be too sure about that. My mind is capable of going beyond the typewriter, you know.'

His vibrant voice was low and she could feel his breath on her cheek. It was an effort to remain calm but she managed to say, 'Actually I didn't know, and I'm beginning to wonder about that fact. You came banging on our door when you realised I could type, and you've proved you'll go to any lengths to keep me at it.'

He regarded her in silence for several moments before his hand on her chin turned her face towards him. 'You don't think there could be more to it than that?' he demanded crisply.

The question caused her to stare at him wonderingly, then she shook her head, smiling in disbelief. 'I doubt it,' she admitted.

'In that case I'll have to convince you.'

She continued to smile. 'Really? How do you propose to do that?'

A sudden movement switched the cushions from behind her back to the end of the divan, and before she realised his intention she found herself lying along its length with her head on the cushion.

'Just relax,' he informed her coolly.

The next instant found him beside her, his right arm with its plaster-covered hand having slipped round her body to hold her against him while his left hand kneaded and fondled the muscles of her back. His head bent and his firm mouth found her lips.

At first the kiss was softly seductive as he teased her lips apart, but slowly and sensuously it deepened to a fierce possessiveness that demanded a response. She found herself unable to argue with its persistent call, and gradually her arms crept about his neck as she gave herself up to the delicious headiness of being wanted by this man.

He did not bother to conceal his urgent need as he leaned over her, pressing her back against the divan. His lips at her throat seemed to sear her skin as they traced a line down towards the rise of her breast, and then his hand crept beneath the low V of her dress to caress her.

Delcie became aware of intense pleasure coursing through her veins, although the sensations of wild desire leaping through every nerve and fibre frightened her into becoming vitally conscious that she was a woman with needs that equalled his own. She was twenty-three, she reminded herself. How much longer must she live without knowing what it was like to make love with a man?

Yet despite the rapture of his kisses which had become almost savage, and the passion vibrating through their bodies, there was a disturbing disquiet at the back of her mind. And as it niggled she told herself she was being a fool. You don't mean a thing to him, common sense warned. You'll satisfy his sexual need, and that will be that. If he loved you it would be different, but, despite this intimacy and these burning kisses, not one word of love has he uttered.

The knowledge was enough to make her wrench her mouth from his and, struggling from his arms, she sat up to gasp, 'Brad, we must stop. We—we're forgetting Amanda.'

He lay perfectly still, then swore softly. 'You're fortunate one of my hands is out of commission, otherwise I'd put you across my knee and spank you for that remark. How can I forget Amanda?'

'You're right,' she sighed. 'How could anyone forget Amanda? She's so beautiful—so vibrant.'

'That's not exactly what I meant,' he said in a voice that sounded like a low growl.

'When you're almost engaged to her you've no right to be kissing me like—like this, or holding me so close,' she admonished, making an effort to get a severe note into her tone.

'Suppose we discuss that point when you see my ring on her finger. It's not there yet, you know. Or is this your way of telling me you're averse to being kissed by a man? Now, be honest.'

She hesitated before admitting, 'Every woman wants to know she's—desirable to a man.'

He chuckled. 'You've no need to worry on that score.'

His arms pulled her against him and as he sought her lips she found herself responding with an ardour she was unable to control. Then, as his hand sought the soft rise beneath the filmy fold of the V-neck, she again felt her breast held in a firm but gentle clasp.

Her heart thumped as desire rose once more and sensations of pleasure again began to tease her body, making her yearn to be close to him, but suddenly she became afraid of her own hunger and of the emotions that were carrying her to the heights where all control would vanish. She knew she had to get a grip on herself, and as his lips began a further sensuous attack on her quivering emotions she spoke in a low voice.

'Amanda's watching you from the shadows.'

He paused, remaining with his arms about her until he said, 'Oh? Mother's standing beside her, I presume?'

Delcie giggled. 'Yes, I believe she is.'

'No doubt they're discussing the dowry—the other half of the property.'

'That's right. Would you like the contract in triplicate?'

'*Damn*!' The expletive broke fiercely. 'You sure know how to throw a bucket of cold water. This would be Aunt Lois's teaching I suppose?' His eyes glared at her through the dim light of the table lamp.

She looked at him frankly. 'Well, she did point out that it was unwise for a girl to allow herself to be used by a man.'

'*Used*? Is that what you think?' His voice had become cold as he moved away from her.

Her eyes became pleading. 'Brad, you know perfectly well we were treading on the edge of dangerous waters. Somebody had to step back, otherwise——' She fell silent, unable to go on.

'Otherwise I'd have dragged you to the bedroom for a session of rape as feared by the aunts. Aunt Alice almost swooned over the thought.' His voice became hard. 'Only it wouldn't be rape, would it? You'd have been a willing partner because you want me as much as I want you. Be honest, admit it,' he ordered.

She stared at him wordlessly, and while she longed to be honest and nod her head she had no intention of allowing him to know she'd yearned for the closest intimacy possible.

He returned her wide-eyed stare grimly, waiting several moments for an answer that did not come. At last he said, 'I think we could do with a cup of coffee. I'll fix it while you stay here and get over the shock of being kissed by a man.'

The words held a sting which told her he considered her to be a stupid little ninny, the irritation bringing her to her feet with a small rush of indignation. 'I'll get the coffee,' she flashed at him. 'You'll have trouble opening the sachets.'

'You're right. When we return I'll see the doctor about getting rid of this plaster. I'm sure it's no longer really necessary, and I'm fed up with it. I want it removed.'

'Don't be too hasty.' She went to the kitchen area, filled the electric jug and took cups from the cupboard. As she did so she knew he paced about the room in a restless manner, and when she placed the steaming coffee on a small table his expression warned that he was still annoyed with her. The reason was not long in being aired.

'I'd like an explanation for your earlier remark.' His tone was knife-edged.

Startled, she was at a momentary loss, but managed to ask casually, 'Which remark do you mean?'

'You suggested I intended *using* you for my own ends.' She was unable to look at him. 'Well, didn't you?'

'Explain yourself,' he snapped.

'Why do we have to talk about it?' she almost entreated.

'Because that remark got under my skin and I'd like to know exactly what you meant by it.'

'Surely it's more than obvious? Despite whatever there is between you and Amanda, you were—you were being particularly nice towards me, but just for your own ends——' She hesitated, unable to continue.

'Go on.' His face had turned into a bleak mask.

'Brad, can't you understand my feelings in this situation—or don't they matter a hoot to you? No, I don't suppose they do,' she added bitterly.

'I'm still waiting for them to be clarified.'

She gulped her coffee while searching for words, and as she put her cup down she said, 'You've indicated that you think I'm stupid, but I'm not so dumb that I imagine you have any depth of feeling for me. Yet you were ready to turn on the big love scene, and to call up anything I might feel for you—but for one reason only.' Her voice had become raised in agitation.

'And that reason is?' he drawled.

'*To get your typing done, of course!*' The words were shouted furiously, then, taking a deep breath, she snatched at control, and as her anger simmered down she explained further. 'In short, you were ready to make phoney love to me so that I'd remain at Bellairs instead of rushing back to Wellington. Now admit that's the truth.'

'Like hell I will! However, I must know what you intend to do. If you're determined to go home I'll have to make arrangements with a public typist.'

'Or with Amanda.' The words slipped out unbidden.

He put his cup down carefully, then turned to look at her. 'Is it possible you could be jealous of Amanda?'

She stared at him, her eyes again wide while a flush of anger rose to her cheeks. 'Me? Jealous of Amanda? That's the most ridiculous thing I've ever heard. Why should I be jealous of Amanda?'

'Why indeed? But one never ceases to wonder at the workings of the female mind.'

'*Jealous of Amanda.*' The words were barely a whisper, muttered furiously to herself.

If he heard them, he ignored them, saying, 'You haven't answered my question about your intentions. Shall I find a public typist, or make arrangements with Amanda—as you've suggested? Or can I rely on you to help with the job? Perhaps you'd rather go to bed and think about it.'

She shook her head. 'No, my mind's made up. I'll stay.'

'Good girl. For a moment I feared my judgment had been way off-base.'

'What do you mean?'

'Well, I'd been so sure I could rely on you.'

She sighed. 'I suppose you can, although I'm afraid the aunts also thought they could rely on me.'

'Ah, yes, but in their case something popped out of the blue to alter things. Have you never realised how the unexpected can overturn the whole course of your intended day? Your plans have been made, something unexpected occurs, and hey presto—the whole day is changed.'

She nodded. 'I know what you mean. Sometimes your whole life is changed, but whether for better or worse is never clear at the moment.'

'Some call it destiny,' he said with a sardonic twist to his lips. Then, with a brisk change of tone, 'Little girl, you've had a busy day. It's time you were in bed. Kiss me goodnight to prove you've come down from your high horse.'

It was an order she had every intention of defying, but because she longed for his kiss she lacked the willpower to rebuff him, so instead of turning away she found herself raising her face to his.

His left arm held her against his body while he nuzzled her ear before tracing a line along her jaw to her throat. Teasing her until he felt her arms tighten about him, his lips then found her own, tasting them sensuously until a deep sigh of yearning escaped her. It was then that he held her from him and spoke tersely.

'Go to bed. And don't be afraid, there's no need to lock your door. When I make love I like to have both hands free.'

She stared at him wordlessly, then went to her room with his last words ringing in her ears. *When he made*

love. Did he make love with Amanda? The thought gave
her a distinct pain, and suddenly the image of the
beautiful brunette lying naked in his arms made her want
to scream with impotent rage.

This intense frustration did not wear off as she lay in
bed. Was she jealous of Amanda? he'd dared to ask. *Was
she ever?* She cringed beneath the sheets at the mere
thought of his guessing just how jealous she was in
reality. There he was, Brad Bellamy, man of property
who needed sons. And there was Amanda, ready and
willing to give them to him.

So why hadn't he married her ages ago? The answer
came clearly. He had been too busy—too involved with
writing books. They had taken his time and his
thoughts—and Amanda would be there when he was
ready for her.

Yet there seemed to be a flaw in this reasoning,
because even her limited experience told Delcie that if
Brad had really wanted to mary Amanda nothing on
earth would have stopped him. They would have been
husband and wife by now. A small moan escaped her as
her thoughts ran riot.

Then she began to ask questions of herself. Why did
this spasm of jealousy engulf her? Naturally it was only a
passing spasm. And why did the image of Amanda lying
in Brad's arms shake her to such an extent?

Surely—surely she couldn't be in love with him? It was
much too soon. She had known him for only a couple of
days. Or could love hit her from out of the blue? No, the
whole question was ridiculous and her trouble was a
mind gone haywire through overtiredness. As he had
said, she'd had a busy day.

She was also overwrought from strain of emotional
stress. There had been all that fuss with her car this
morning, followed by the misery of being personally
driven home to Wellington—or so she had thought at the
time. And then there had been the shock of coming to
Otaki where even watching the tape recorder had had its

moments of tension when she had found it necessary to take note of rapidly spoken Scottish words that could later be difficult to decipher.

Memory of the katipo spider crept into her mind, causing her to shudder. Thank God she had seen it in time. And then a smile touched her soft lips as she recalled his attentions towards her during dinner when his eyes had hardly left her face.

'I suppose you know you're something to catch the eye Delcie,' was all he had said by way of a compliment.

Later had come the joy—yes, she had to admit to it being a joy—of feeling his arms about her, the closeness of his body and his lips upon her own. And even if the embrace had been a one-armed affair she had been vitally aware of the desire pulsing through his body. It had put her into a state of yearning that had made her breath quicken and her entire being tingle.

Was this the sort of thing that had happened to her mother? she wondered. Aunt Alice had been the one to let slip the fact that 'that fellow' seemed to have appeared from out of the blue and had swept poor silly Denise off her feet in two days flat.

Two days? Delcie frowned as she stared into the darkness, was history repeating itself? The thoughts swirling about in her mind kept her awake for a long time.

Next day the journey home was taken at speed, although a stop was made for lunch. The small cafeteria provided a salad, and as they sat at a table Brad looked at her critically.

'You have shadows beneath your eyes,' he told her bluntly.

'You're telling me nicely that I'm baggy-eyed?'

'Not exactly, but you look tired. Didn't you sleep well?'

'I did eventually, but I lay awake for ages.'

His gaze became penetrating. 'Why? You were regretting your decision to stay?'

'No, it wasn't that——' Her voice trailed away.

'Then what was it?' His tone had become insistent.

It was impossible to meet his eyes and she could only stare at the food on her plate while she raked through her mind for an answer, at last she said. 'Your mother won't be at all pleased when she sees me return with you, and as for Amanda——'

'The thought of them gives you the jitters?'

She nodded silently, thankful to have found a reason for her sleeplessness that could indeed be a fact.

'Suppose you leave them both to me. Just seat yourself at the typewriter and forget about them.'

She laughed as her hand flicked an imaginary switch in the air. 'Whip—whip—You're quite a slave driver.'

'That confounded deadline worries me,' he admitted gloomily. 'I prefer to write a book at leisure, rather than with a finishing date hovering over my head like a black cloud.'

She sent him a bright smile. 'Cheer up, you'll make it in time with me to help you.'

He regarded her in silence for several long moments. 'Bless you, Delcie,' he muttered huskily at last.

His tone and the look in his brown eyes filled her with satisfaction, and when they continued the journey she felt more relaxed as she sat in the comfortably shaped seats of the smart grey car. A slight smile played about her lips as she listened to the soothing music coming from a radio cassette, and for the moment everything seemed to be right in her world—except that the miles were disappearing behind them much too quickly.

The return to Bellairs was not helped by the sight of Joan and Amanda reclining in wicker chairs on a shaded part of the front verandah. And when Brad stopped the Renault beside the wide concrete steps, both women rose to their feet to stare in silence at Delcie.

Joan, slim and elegant in a tailored summer dress, was the first to speak. 'You've come back?'

Brad answered her. 'Your eyesight does you credit, Mother.'

Amanda spoke stonily, her tone indicating she was making an effort to control her anger. 'Do you mean to say you took her all the way to Wellington, and then brought her back?'

'Persuaded her to come back would be closer,' he informed her blandly. 'I decided I can't possibly get the book finished in time without her help.'

Delcie got out of the car and stood looking at the two women at the top of the steps. The thought of allowing them to believe a lie—that they had been to Wellington—niggled at her, so she decided to be honest. 'Brad didn't take me home,' she admitted. 'We've been to Otaki.'

'*Otaki?*' Joan echoed faintly.

'That's right.' Brad grinned. 'I think I told you I had Otaki in mind. Old Jock Mackenzie and his wife have retired to a warmer climate than the south's high country. His sheepdog stories are really good value.'

Delcie snatched at the opportunity to escape. Using his statement as an excuse, she said. 'I'd like to make a start on those tapes while some of his broad Scottish words are still in my mind.'

'A good idea,' he agreed. 'I'll come and listen while you work on them. Perhaps we can decipher some of the more difficult ones together.' He paused, his eyes sweeping over her with a light of concern. 'You're sure you're not feeling too tired?'

Amanda's irritation reached breaking point, her voice snapping angrily as she spoke to Brad. 'Personally I consider it high time you dropped this stupid book-writing racket and settled down to running your property. You shouldn't leave everything to staff.'

He remained calm as he drawled, 'Is that a fact, Mandy, old girl? Well, *personally*, I consider it high time you minded your own business.'

She was quick to see her mistake and to apologise.

'You're right, Brad—of course you're right. It's not my business and I'm sorry. I know your writing is important to you—I know it's a bug that has really bitten you, and we're all very proud of what you've achieved.'

He accepted the olive branch, then said drily, 'Thank you for the kind words, Amanda. And speaking of bugs——' He told them about the katipo, then added, 'So you see, if it hadn't been for Delcie it could've been curtains for me.'

In the silence that followed his words he carried the tape recorder towards the office while Delcie followed him like an obedient child. She was aware that Joan Bellamy wore a worried frown, and she could almost feel sharp arrows piercing her back as Amanda's glinting eyes followed her into the hall.

But their attitude was only something she had expected, and she knew she would have to learn to cope with it, the easiest way being to ignore it, so a smile on her face kept her discomfort hidden from Brad as he placed the tape recorder beside the typewriter.

When she settled down to work she found that the slow deliberate speech of Jock Mackenzie made it easy for her to keep up with the flow of words. As her fingers flew over the keys she felt thankful that, despite teaching others, she had kept up her own typing speed, and that she had the ability to transfer the words from the tape to paper so rapidly.

She also knew that Brad watched her as he listened from the depths of the armchair, and during one pause when she switched the tape back to check a difficult word she turned to find his eyes resting upon her. There was an unfathomable expression within their depths, and the reason for it was not a secret.

'I can see you're definitely a career girl,' he said. 'I don't think country life would suit you at all. In fact, I'm having second thoughts about taking you to meet Richard Dillon.'

'Oh? Why?'

'It would be a pity if the poor fellow really did become emotionally involved, only to see you flit back to the city.'

'Nobody's likely to become emotionally involved,' she assured him. Least of all yourself, she added silently as she sent the tape forward again.

His voice came over the electric hum of the typewriter. 'Are you annoyed about something?'

She stopped the tape. 'Of course not. Why should I be annoyed?'

'You appear to be hammering the keys. There's no need, you know.'

Heavens, was she so transparent? Thinking quickly she said, 'Perhaps I'm a little disappointed. I was looking forward to meeting the present owner of my parents' home. However, if you'd rather not take me, I'll go alone,' she added on a defiant note.

He regarded her in silence until he said, 'I've just had an idea. Mother can arrange a pre-Christmas party and she can invite the Dillons. Did you realise that Christmas is less than four weeks away?'

'Yes. It'll be the first Christmas I've spent away from the aunts. It's usually been very quiet, perhaps in a motel or wherever we've been having the famous yearly holiday.'

'This year you can experience a home Christmas. Mother likes to turn on all the trimmings with roast turkey and Christmas pud, even if the day is sweltering. Amanda always helps her decorate the Christmas tree. It's a yearly ritual.'

Which Amanda expects to carry on for *your* children, Delcie thought. Aloud she said, 'Amanda appears to spend a great deal of her time here. Or is this my imagination?'

'No. Mother and Amanda are wrapped up in each other.'

'Perhaps it's not surprising. They're similar in appearance, both being tall, slim and dark—almost like mother and daughter. I can understand your mother's hopes——'

'Let's get on with the job,' he cut in, his tone clipped.

The suggestion of a pre-Christmas party was made that evening at dinner when Brad said to his mother, 'Don't you think it's time the Dillons were offered a drink in this house? I'd like Delcie to meet Richard.'

'What a marvellous idea,' applauded the ever-present Amanda. She turned to Delcie, her face alight with enthusiasm. 'You'll like Richard—he's such a nice person. He's handsome and unmarried, so what more could any girl ask for?' she added with a gay laugh.

Delcie knew exactly what more she could ask for, but the information was kept to herself. Nor was she bubbling with joy at the thought of meeting Richard Dillon—even if he now owned her parents' property— because this meant that Brad himself had no serious thoughts towards her. Otherwise he wouldn't be so keen for them to meet, would he.

She was being a fool to allow her thoughts and emotions to turn towards Brad, she told herself. How could she possibly expect him to look once—much less twice—at her when he had Amanda? When comparing herself with the beautiful brunette, she felt pale and insignificant, like a glass of still white wine standing beside sparkling red burgundy.

For the rest of the evening she sat listening while catering was discussed, and the names of guests were suggested and listed by Amanda. She'd be a stranger in a room full of people, she realised gloomily. Apart from Brad, his mother and Amanda, she wouldn't know a soul——She was startled by the mention of a name that was familiar.

'We'd better invite old Luke Pringle.' Brad said.

'Yes, of course,' Joan agreed. 'He's a dear man and so reliable.'

Delcie hesitated, then asked, 'Do you mean Mr Pringle, the solicitor?'

Amanda showed surprise with a small laugh. 'Are you trying to imply that you know him?'

She hesitated again. 'I can't say I really know him because I've met him only once. He was my father's solicitor. He attended to my parents' estate.' A troubled look crept into her eyes. 'I must admit I feel terribly guilty about him. I should've been to see him ages ago, at least to thank him for—for handling my affairs.'

Amanda's laugh rang more clearly. 'Really? Your *affairs*? How very important that sounds.'

'Oh, they're not big,' Delcie hastened to assure her.

'But certainly better than nothing,' Brad put in drily. 'Over the years old Luke will have been investing on Delcie's behalf money paid for the property.' He cocked an eyebrow at her. 'Am I right?'

She nodded. 'Well, yes—he's been most helpful——'

'Oh, I see——' Amanda's eyes widened as she sat up and looked at Delcie with new respect. It was almost as though she was saying she'd have to reverse her assumption of Delcie being a penniless go-getter whose sole aim had been to captivate Brad Bellamy.

Delcie sensed the change of attitude. Her heart lifted and suddenly she began to look forward to the party where she would meet the Dillons who had known her parents——And Mr Pringle would be there, too.

Amanda's voice cut in on her thoughts. 'It's *ages* since I last saw Richard. I'm really looking forward to seeing him again. We danced so well together at the last hunt ball. He waltzes beautifully, and we just seemed to float round the room.'

She's trying to make Brad jealous, Delcie thought.

'Shall we dance at the party—perhaps out on the verandah?' Amanda pursued. 'I'd like to dance with Richard again,' she added with a brief glance at Brad.

'We'll dance if it's not too not,' he told her. Then turning to Delcie, he asked, 'Do you like dancing?'

'Oh yes, I love it.' Would he dance with her she wondered, or would he be too busy attending to guests?

As she looked at him her eyes shone, almost revealing her thoughts.

A swift glance passed from Amanda to Joan. 'I'm sure you'll find Richard monopolising your time,' Joan said with a hint of satisfaction. 'As Amanda says, he's a very good dancer.'

'Yes, I'm afraid that will be the case,' Brad added with casual ease. 'I quite expect Richard to sweep you right off your feet.'

Delcie stared down at the table. And you couldn't care less about that, she decided miserably.

CHAPTER SIX

As she lay in bed an hour later, thoughts on the party invaded Delcie's mind, and mingled with them was the memory of the day she had met Mr Pringle. She had been in her late teens and still terrified of Aunt Lois when he had paid an unexpected visit to the house in Karori. The purpose of his visit had been to assure himself of her well-being, and to discuss financial matters, but this was something she had not understood until later.

Nor had she seen much of the sparse-haired solicitor on that particular day, because Aunt Lois had bustled her out of the room, declaring that Mr Pringle had business to discuss with *her*. The fact of it being Delcie's own business that was being discussed seemed to be beside the point, and even now she almost quailed as she recalled Aunt Lois's foaming rage when he had left with a grim look on his face.

Later Delcie had dared to ask timidly, 'Was Mr Pringle annoyed about something?'

Lois had brushed the query aside. 'Oh no, we were just discussing your household expenses. Men don't seem to know much about the cost of running a home.'

Delcie had been surprised. '*My* household expenses?' It was the first time she had realised she possessed such encumbrances.

'Of course you have expenses, child,' Aunt Lois had informed her impatiently. 'One doesn't have a roof over one's head without cost. Rates have to be paid to the City Council, and there's the electricity burned while you practice your endless typing. There's the telephone account, the television licence and all that food a growing girl eats. Naturally I attend to these matters from the cheques Mr Pringle sends.'

'What was it he said about milking the child?' Aunt Alice asked nervously.

'Be quiet, Alice,' Lois had snapped, 'The man's a fool. He even had the temerity to point out that as we own the house the maintenance expenses should be shared. I told him quite smartly that after all we'd done for Delcie we were due for a little consideration where money is concerned. Isn't that so, dear?'

Delcie recalled the pale blue eyes glaring at her. All she had been able to do was nod her head and say, 'Yes, Aunt Lois.'

But Mr Pringle's visit had brought about a change, and the next cheque to arrive had been half the usual amount with one portion being placed in an account intended for Delcie's sole use. The accompanying note had explained that, as her late father's executor, Mr Pringle considered she had now reached the age of handling at least some of her own money.

Delcie recalled that Aunt Lois had been livid. In fact Aunt Alice had feared she might suffer a stroke. However, she had got over her rage and life had gone along as usual, except that Delcie was now able to make purchases without having to ask Aunt Lois for a few dollars of her own money.

Thinking back to those late teenage years, she realised that her improved financial state had also done much to bring about a subtle change within herself. She no longer felt like a destitute waif who relied upon Aunt Lois's bounty, and gradually she had found the courage to assert her own personality. Fortunately it had developed sufficiently to enable her to defy Aunt Lois when Brad Bellamy had knocked at the door to demand her help, because without it she knew she would never have come away with him.

Next morning she went to the office to begin work in earnest and as her fingers tapped the keys the words hidden on the narrow black tapes became readable as they flowed on to the white paper in the typewriter. There were few interruptions, apart from Sally who brought in mid-morning coffee or afternoon tea, or from Joan who smiled vaguely from the doorway as she asked if there was anything she needed

Delcie merely shook her head, although she could have told Joan that yes, there was something she needed. It was the sight of Brad, who appeared to be avoiding the office, and with each passing day of that week she knew she needed him more and more.

Granted, she saw him briefly at meal times, or in the distance with Amanda, who seemed to have developed the habit of clinging to his arm. However, this served only to frustrate her, stirring the craving to have a few intimate moments of his company, but as these did not appear to be forthcoming she had no option but to keep on with the job and to control her inner fretting.

By Friday she had completed every tape in the drawer and she was just stretching her back when Sally came in with afternoon tea.

'You're lucky to be able to type like that,' the girl said wistfully. 'I wish I could do something more important than housework. It's just—just nothing.'

'The job you do is very important,' Delcie assured her. 'Your mother and Mrs Bellamy need your help. Have you never realised just how important it is to be *needed*?'

'I've never thought of it like that.'

'Did you know I teach typing, Sally? If you'd really like to learn to type I could soon show you how to go about it.'

But Sally shook her head. 'If I learnt to type I'd want to find a job in Masterton and that'd mean leaving here. I feel safe here with Mum and Mrs Bellamy, and *he's* always so kind to me. He always gives me a lovely Christmas present.'

Delcie's mind lurched. *Christmas presents*. She'd hardly given them a thought and suddenly she knew she must find gifts for this household, and for Amanda. But what on earth could she give Brad?

Sally said, 'All the parcels are put round the tree: big ones at the bottom while little ones are tied to the branches among the lights and decorations.' She sent a swift glance towards the door then lowered her voice. 'Brad and Amanda are in Masterton at this very minute. Mum says they're doing Christmas shopping. She says Mrs Bellamy's quite excited about it.'

Delcie's spirits took an instinctive downward dive. 'Oh? Why should she be excited over Christmas shopping?'

'Because she's hoping he'll buy Amanda an engagement ring, of course. Mum says they're probably choosing it together. Lord knows he's been long enough in getting round to it.'

Delcie's heart sank to an even lower level, and to hide her dismay she began making neat piles of the typed pages, leaving each with its individual tape resting on top. At the same time she told herself she was being a fool to listen to Sally's gossip, although it was impossible to prevent the knife wound caused by the thought of Brad placing a ring on Amanda's finger.

However, when Brad returned from town he was alone, so there was no way of being able to see signs of excitement, suppressed or otherwise, in Amanda's eyes.

'I've finished the tapes,' she told him, searching his face for signs of a newly engaged man, but, apart from a satisfied look as he regarded the stacks of typewritten sheets, his expression told her nothing.

'Good girl,' he approved. 'I'll make a start on editing them this evening.' He turned and unexpectedly snatched her to him, kissing her swiftly and pressing her breasts against him. Then, almost before she could catch her breath, he released her abruptly and left the room.

She stood immobile, touching her lips lightly and still feeling the brief but firm pressure of his mouth. That's not the action of a newly engaged man, she thought, and suddenly she felt happier.

Later, when coffee was wheeled into the lounge, Delcie noticed that Brad failed to join them. She went to the trolley and poured two cups and as she handed one to Joan the older woman said,

'I think Brad is in the office. I suppose he's going over all that work you've done for him.' She sipped her coffee thoughtfully, then added, 'I'm surprised Amanda didn't come home with him. They were shopping today, you know.'

Delcie showed polite interest. 'Oh? Christmas shopping, I suppose?'

'Yes. I really expected——' she fell silent.

'You expected——' She kept her tone guarded as she waited for Joan to tell her more.

'Do you think they could have quarrelled?' Joan asked abruptly. 'You were in the office with Brad. How did he seem to you?'

Delcie recalled the brief kiss in the office, then looked into her cup as she said carefully, 'I'm afraid I haven't known him long enough to understand his moods. Don't forget, I met him only a week ago today.'

'That's long enough for some people to become very close,' Joan retorted, staring at Delcie with a hint of suspicion.

Delcie forced herself to smile. 'I can assure you that Brad and I haven't become close this week. I've hardly seen him since we returned from Otaki. I can only presume he's been spending the time with Amanda,' she added with a cheerfulnes she did not feel.

'Nothing of the sort,' Joan retorted. 'He's been out on the farm. He does spend a certain amount of time out there, you know.'

'No, Mrs Bellamy, I wouldn't know,' Delcie pointed out frankly.

Joan's voice took on a plaintive note. 'Poor Amanda. She's spent hours waiting for him to come in because naturally she likes to see him each day. I do hope they haven't quarrelled,' she added, a worried frown creasing her brow as she stared at Delcie.

'What would they quarrel about.' Delcie asked carefully, then immediately regretted the question.

'Well—yourself, of course,' Joan declared, her voice plainly accusing. 'After all, he said he was driving you back to Wellington. But did he do so? *No*. Instead he took you to a motel in Otaki. Isn't that enough to rile a girl who expects to marry him?'

Delcie sighed, then decided to speak frankly. 'Mrs Bellamy, as Brad's mother you *must* know that, despite your own wishes or Amanda's expectations, he'll do exactly as he himself desires. He's a determined man with a strong mind of his own. I'll never forget the shock of his arrival at our house when he asked me to come to Bellairs to help him. And it wasn't a request; it was a demand.'

'He was always stubborn as a small boy,' Joan reminisced fondly. 'He persisted until he got exactly what he wanted, and he hasn't changed over the years.'

Delcie smiled. 'Doesn't that tell you anything?'

Joan glanced at her sharply. 'What are you trying to say?'

'Well, it seems to me that if he'd wanted Amanda to be his wife—if he really *loved* her—they'd have been married ages ago.'

Joan looked at her coldly. 'Are you suggesting that I've been living in a fool's world of wishful thinking?'

Delcie's face still held a smile although it had now become somewhat forced. She had no intention of arguing with Joan Bellamy. Therefore she said quietly, 'Those are your words, not mine. Mrs Bellamy, However, it's possible——'

The older woman's tone continued to be icy. 'Have you any further comments to make concerning this household?'

'Oh no, it's not my place to do so.' Delcie sipped her coffee thoughtfully. She longed to point out that if Brad married Amanda his mother might find herself in a very different position from the one she was now enjoying. In fact she might find herself removed to a flat in Masterton so quickly she'd wonder how she got there.

She also had a strong conviction that, despite the apparent closeness between Joan Bellamy and Amanda, the kudos of being mistress of Bellairs would not be handed over lightly, nor would Amanda agree to take second place in the home for which she had waited so long and so patiently.

Joan watched her closely. 'What's going on in that mind of yours?' she asked with what appeared to be forced lightness. 'Please understand that my own mind is not so closed it's unable to listen to the opinion of others.'

But Delcie shook her head, feeling it wiser to change the subject. 'May I pour you another cup of coffee?' she asked. Then, having filled the cup that was handed to her she said, 'It's still nice and hot. Do you think I should take Brad's coffee to him.'

Joan sighed. 'Yes. He'll be so engrossed he'll have forgotten about coffee. Really, I wish I knew why Mandy didn't come home with him this evening——'

Delcie made her escape. She carried the coffee along the hall, walking slowly to avoid spilling it in the saucer, her feet making no sound on the thick carpet. However, as she reached the office door she was brought to an abrupt halt by a sight that filled her with surprise. Brad sat at the workbench, a sheet of paper before him. He was writing busily, and it was only then that she realised that he was *left-handed*.

She entered the room and placed the coffee beside him. 'I see you can write. I had no idea you're left-handed.' Her voice rang with barely concealed accusation.

He stood up and turned to face her. 'No? Well the subject didn't come up did it?'

'You might have told me.' Her tone betrayed the fact that she felt aggrieved.

'Why? What difference does it make?'

'For some odd reason I feel as though I've been tricked.'

'Are you suggesting that something's been put across you? Please remember that, even if I can write, I certainly can't type. And that's the job that has to be done.' His manner changed as he added, 'Anyhow, it's good to have a strong left hand' His arm went out to encircle her waist, and as he drew her against him he kissed her with an intensity that sent the blood pounding up into her temples.

She longed to remain leaning against him, to feel the pressure of his arm about her and to respond to his kisses, but to what purpose? They were only superficial caresses that would break her heart if she took them seriously. And then the image of Joan Bellamy rose before her mind, terrifying her and causing her to gasp, 'Brad, *please*—your mother might see us.'

'So what?' The question came nonchalantly.

'You know perfectly well there'd be hell to pay. She's disappointed enough as it is, and to see us like this would give her reason to throw me out of the house.'

He chuckled. 'Are you saying she'd throw *my* secretary

out of *my* house? You've got to be joking. She wouldn't do that.'

'I'm sure she'd have a good try. Really, Brad, I'm quite serious. She thinks—well, I couldn't possibly tell you what she thinks.' Embarrassment caused her to fall silent.

'You must imagine I'm mighty dumb,' he said mockingly. 'I know exactly what she thinks. But what's this business about her being disappointed?'

Delcie turned away from him, and, moving towards the window, she stood staring across the lawn.

He became impatient. 'Come on, if you know she's disappointed you must also know why.'

She knew an answer of some sort was expected, so she said hesitatingly, 'I—I think she expected you and Amanda to—to visit a jeweller's shop today.'

His brows shot up. 'She did? Well, to be honest I did happen to visit Masterton's main jeweller today.' The admission came almost reluctantly.

She swung round to face him, her eyes clouded by a sudden anguish. 'You did? You've come home—engaged to Amanda?'

He shook his head. 'Certainly not. Is that what Mother was expecting?'

'Yes. But Amanda didn't even come home with you and now she fears you may have quarrelled.'

He gave a short laugh. 'I'll admit that Amanda is not particularly pleased with me at the moment.'

'Oh? Why?' She looked at him expectantly, her curiosity aroused. 'Did you quarrel?'

But he did not enlighten her. Instead he turned to indicate the stacks of typewritten sheets. 'I'm making a start on these pages by sorting and combining the sections that belong to each other. It's good to have so many authentic anecdotes about the seeing-eye dogs for the blind. Nor did I realise I had so much about the police dogs. I was afraid sheepdogs would dominate the book, but fortunately it's well balanced with other breeds.'

Delcie realised he was deliberately getting away from the subject of Amanda, so she complied by saying, 'I loved the story of Joe, the roamer, and also the lovely one about the kleptomaniac spaniel that stole everything he could possibly carry home to his kennel.'

They then discussed the pattern of work for the coming week and by mutual consent the subject of Amanda was dropped from the conversation. Not that this prevented Delcie from wondering what had caused the rift between them. Had she herself been the reason, as Joan Bellamy had suggested?

The days that followed were spent in quiet communication as they worked side by side in the office. Little explanation was necessary for her to understand that extracts from her own recently typed pages had to be redrafted into publishable form and then added to chapters already written, and it was during a coffee break that she asked a question that had been niggling at her.

'I can't help wondering why chapters have been typed before all the material has been collected.'

'It's because one is never sure when all the available material *has* been collected, or if more will come to light. One can't wait for ever, so one gets on with the job with what has already been found.'

'That's easy to understand,' she said, thinking of the material recently taken off the tape recorder. But what she didn't understand had nothing to do with the book's content. Instead it concerned Amanda, who had become conspicuous by her absence. And when several days had passed without a sign of her presence in the house Delcie became even more puzzled.

On Friday morning she was unable to resist remarking upon the fact to Brad. 'Do you realise that Amanda hasn't been here for days?' she asked.

He shrugged. 'Hasn't she? I hadn't noticed. She'll turn up. She always does.' His tone became clipped as he closed the subject by writing busily.

'You certainly take her for granted,' Delcie retorted, strangely irritated on Amanda's behalf.

He ignored the remark.

A short time later the mid-morning coffee, usually carried in by Sally, was placed beside them by Joan. She was smartly dressed in a silk suit for town and as she carefully pushed papers aside for the tray she said, 'I'm going to Masterton to do my Christmas shopping. I'm meeting Amanda for lunch and we're going to that new place people say is so good. Perhaps she'll explain why she's been keeping away from us all this week.'

'Perhaps.' Brad's tone was non-committal.

Joan's eyes sent an accusing glance towards Delcie, then rested upon Brad, a question lurking within their depths. Her voice was aggrieved as she spoke to him. 'Tell me, Brad, have you quarrelled with Amanda?'

He laughed as he drawled, 'Some people would call it a lover's tiff, Mother, others would say it was a clash of wills.'

'I see.' She stared at him silently for several moments, torn between understanding for her own son and sympathy for Amanda until at last she said, 'The poor girl—she's probably very upset. I'd like to know what it's all about.'

'All you have to do is wring it out of her. It shouldn't be too hard.' His eyes held a strange glint.

But Joan was persistent. 'I can't remember when she has stayed away for so long.'

'Good grief, Mother, she practically lives here.'

Delcie tried to put in a cheerful word. 'I'm sure she'll be back soon, Mrs Bellamy, especially as you're having lunch with her. After all, it's only five days since she was here.'

Joan glared at her. 'Five days? Brad and Amanda should've been married five *years* ago.'

Brad heaved a large sigh to indicate his extreme patience. He stood up, took his mother's arm and led her to the door. 'Please calm down, Mother, dear. You'll only tire yourself before you set out. You know you've got a big day's shopping ahead of you. Now then, have you got your cheque book and all your credit cards?'

'Kindly stop treating me as though I'm almost senile,' she snapped at him as she flounced from the room.

Moments later they heard the red Toyota roar past the verandah door, and although Delcie waited for Brad to say something about the cause of his mother's irritation, no comment came. His flying pen seemed to indicate that he was throwing himself into the task with extra vigour, although it was not as if he had worked with any less speed during the week.

Nor had there been any intimacy during those days, Delcie recalled sadly. There had been no snatched kisses, no unexpected feel of his arms about her, and although she had craved for a few moments of tenderness their relationship had been kept to a strictly casual basis. Was this something to do with Amanda? she wondered. Perhaps he was grieving silently for her and was therefore determined to become thoroughly engrossed.

The day passed quickly with little time spared for lunch, and as they returned to the office he paused to regard her intently. 'I dare say you've decided I'm a slave-driver of the worst type.'

She returned his gaze steadily. 'I thought the all-important object was to get the job finished.'

He tipped her chin and stared down into her face, and for one delirious moment she imagined he was about to kiss her. But he did not. He merely said, 'And when that time comes you'll jump into your car and race back to Wellington, joyfully blowing the horn all the way.'

'That's what *you* think,' she said, unaware of the utter dejection in her voice. How could she tell him she hated the thought of leaving Bellairs—that she'd even brave his mother's antagonism for the sake of remaining at his side?

It was late afternoon when the red Toyota swept past the side verandah door on its return from town. It was followed closely by Amanda's yellow Austin Mini, and as the two vehicles went to the back of the house Brad grinned but said nothing. Watching him from the corner of her eye, Delcie guessed he was saying a silent *I thought so* to himself.

Joan came in a few minutes later, her mood obviously much brighter than it had been before she'd left for town. 'Guess who's here,' she exclaimed with a touch of gaiety.

'Impossible for me to do so.' Brad's tone was sardonic.

'I persuaded Amanda to come home for evening meal. And that's not all,' she went on happily. 'We've made arrangements for tomorrow.'

He looked at her sharply. 'You have? What sort of arrangements, may I ask?'

'We'll discuss it when you've poured our drinks,' replied his mother, as though determined to keep him in suspense. Then, smiling brightly first at Delcie and then at Brad, she left the room.

Delcie was filled with curiosity, but not for the world would she admit it. Also, a strange instinct seemed to warn her that Joan Bellamy's elated mood had something to do with herself, although this, she decided firmly, could be only her imagination.

Watching Brad as he continued to write, she realised he was in no hurry to leave the office, nor did he appear to be particularly anxious to learn the nature of the arrangements that had been made. However, the time came when he laid down his pen and made a leisurely way towards the living-room.

Amanda was there, looking as chic as ever, and Delcie was more than surprised by the dark-eyed girl's unexpected show of friendliness towards her. She also noticed that Brad was treated to a deliberate coolness, but he appeared to ignore it as he handed round the sherry-filled glasses.

At last he said, 'Well, Mother, what's all this excitement that's almost bubbling out of you?'

A look passed between Amanda and Joan as the latter said, 'We're taking Delcie for a drive tomorrow.'

'Oh? You're sure she wants to go with you?' His clipped tone had a knife-cutting edge.

'She'll come, all right.' Amanda's voice rang with confidence. 'We're taking her to see her old home.'

Delcie was startled. She sat up straight, her blue eyes wide with surprise as she stared at Amanda. She didn't really want to visit her old home in the company of these people; she longed to go there alone, to walk about the place trying to remember. But this, she realised, would also be impossible, because the present owner would be there.

Amanda's voice echoed with satisfaction. 'The arrangements were easily made,' she told Brad. 'It was just as though it was meant to happen. There we were, sitting at our lunch table, when along came Richard Dillon. He sat down and joined us. I'd forgotten how very handsome he is. He's matured into a rugged outdoor type and is enough to make any girl's heart flip over.'

Delcie looked at Amanda in silence. She could have said her own heart had already flipped over, and that for her things would never be the came again.

'I can't understand why he's never married,' Amanda exclaimed with some force. 'Really, I find him to be charming.'

'Perhaps he's waiting for the right girl to come along,' Joan smiled. She sent a side glance towards Delcie as she added, 'We're driving there after lunch tomorrow.'

That's what you think,' Brad scowled. 'Delcie and I have work to do. We're up to our necks in it.'

'But it's Saturday and you've had Delcie working all the week,' his mother pointed out. 'She needs a rest.'

Amanda chimed in, 'I'm longing to see Richard's house. 'I've heard he's interested in antiques. As for Richard himself, I assure you he's just like a film star—one of those handsome men out of a western.'

Delcie wanted to laugh. She could see through Amanda's tactics, even if the others were unable to do so. All this raving on about Richard Dillon was merely a ploy to make Brad jealous. But was she succeeding? A quick peep towards the end of the table told her that Brad was not at all amused. His dark brows were drawn together in a frown, and there was a hint of hardness about his mouth. Yes, it seemed obvious that Amanda's words were getting to him, and Delcie's own heart sank a little as she suspected that perhaps Brad was somewhat shaken by Amanda's unexpected interest in Richard.

As for herself, she was finding difficulty in believing that she'd see her old home in as short a time as tomorrow. The knowledge filled her with an inner excitement she found hard to suppress, yet she was also conscious of other emotions. Suppose she made an utter fool of herself by being unable to control tears when she saw the house? Amananda would be highly amused. And worse still, suppose Richard guessed the matchmaking plans these people had in mind? She would die of embarrassment.

And then Aunt Lois's words slid into her memory. Don't go digging up skeletons, she had advised. The recollection mingled with the thoughts whirling around in Delcie's mind, giving her the urge to walk outside where the fresh air might clear her head, so when dinner was finished she escaped to the garden.

The long summer evening had not yet darkened, and as she wandered along the side path the fragrance of roses drew her towards the front of the house. Perhaps it was the memory of Brad's embrace beneath the rose-covered archway that caused her steps to turn in that direction, but suddenly the sound of voices brought her to an abrupt halt.

Amanda's laughter, followed by the deep tones of Brad's voice, told her they were in the garden near the archway. Was he holding her close beneath it? Delcie felt she couldn't bear to come face to face with them, so she turned and hurried back to the house. Obviously the tiff between them had now vanished, she decided, and as she went upstairs to her room she felt devoured by jealousy.

Next morning work in the office continued as usual, although Delcie was still gripped by an excitement that made concentration difficult. She took stealthy peeps at Brad, but if he had come to any special understanding with Amanda during the previous evening, he failed to show any sign of it.

Head down, he wrote rapidly as he prepared the material for her to type, and although they heard Amanda's car go past the verandah door he neither looked up nor uttered a comment. It was then she began to wonder if he was annoyed because she was going with his mother and Amanda. Did he consider she was walking out on the job?

Watching him covertly, a silent plea formed in her mind. Please Brad don't be annoyed with me. Then, asserting herself, she added, because if you are, that's just too bad. I'm going with them, so there!

The thought made her leave the office and run lightly upstairs to her room where she changed from her jeans into an apricot dress with a matching jacket. When she returned, he glanced at her but still said nothing, and not until they were sitting at lunch did she learn of his plans.

'I've decided to come with you,' he informed his mother.

'That'll be nice, dear,' Joan smiled. 'I'm sure Richard will be pleased. You haven't seen him for ages.'

Amanda sent him a direct look from across the table. 'There's no real need for you to come if you'd rather remain with all those dogs you've got on paper. I'm quite capable of driving Joan and Delcie to visit Richard.'

'We'll go in the Renault,' he said. 'I'm sure Delcie hasn't fogotten that I've already mentioned taking her to see the place. In fact I believed I said I'd make it this Saturday.'

His mother looked at him reproachfully. 'This is the first I've heard of it,' she pointed out.

'I hadn't found time to get in touch with Richard,' he explained.

Delcie felt she had to let him know she understood. 'You mind has been so engrossed,' she excused.

His brown eyes regarded her steadily. 'But you do remember I made you a promise?'

'Of course, and I knew you'd keep it sooner or later.' The smile she sent him was full of confidence. She was also glad he had decided to accompany them. Her spirits rose, causing a quiet inner happiness that made her eyes shine like sun on deep water.

It was after two o'clock when they left. Joan Bellamy sat in front beside Brad, while Amanda and Delcie occupied the back seat. The road was flat during the few miles between Masterton and Carterton, but when it left the main highway to run westward towards the Tararua ranges it undulated between low hills which reached higher levels as they drew nearer the mountain foothills.

The passing scene of green fields grazed by sheep and cattle gave Delcie a feeling of unreality as she thought that, but for the death of her parents, this would have been her own background. She knew this was not the first time she had been driven over this same road, although she was unable to recall any part of it.

Almost as though reading her thoughts, Brad caught her eye in the rear vision mirror. 'I wonder if you'll remember anything at all?' he said with a touch of kindness.

She shook her head. 'I doubt it, although I seem to imagine there was a swing. It hung from the branch of a tree growing near a gate.'

'You don't remember the house?' Amanda asked.

'Not even remotely. After all, I was only three.'

'Keep your eyes open,' said Brad. 'You'll see it round the next bend—over to the left——'

She leaned forward, her eyes searching among the trees on the far hillside for a first glimpse of her old home. A red roof and a flash of white timbers caught her vision, and as they approached she knew she must get a grip on her emotions. She must not make an idiot of herself by weeping.

CHAPTER SEVEN

THE first real test for Delcie's control was nearer than she had expected, because within the next few moments Brad stopped the car and pointed to one of the pillars flanking the entrance to the drive. 'Do you see what they call the place?' he asked, turning to look at her.

She stared at the name set in the concrete. '*Linden?*' she whispered. 'It's—it's almost like a memorial.'

Joan turned to look at her kindly, perhaps understanding how she felt. 'Richard's parents were friends of your own parents,' she reminded her. 'Does it make you feel as though you've come home?'

Delcie shook her head, the lump in her throat almost choking her. 'No, not really.'

Amanda said, 'I think I was wonderful of Richard to have kept the name. He could have changed it for anything of his own choosing. I told you, he's something quite special.'

Delcie looked at her curiously. Was this part of her campaign to make Brad jealous? If so, wasn't she overdoing it a little? She glanced at Brad, trying to judge the effect of Amanda's words on him but he gave no sign that he had even heard them.

The drive curved uphill for a short distance before reaching the house, and as it came into view Delcie was pleasantly surprised by the sight of the building which, although two-storeyed, was not large. 'It has an air of stability about it,' she remarked, uttering her first impression. 'I love those dormer windows.'

'It's typical of the houses built before the turn of the

century,' Brad explained. 'Only the best timber was used.'

'I love it! It's a period piece,' exclaimed Amanda, her voice echoing an unexpected enthusiasm.

Joan turned swiftly to send her a look of surprise. 'One would almost imagine you prefer it to Bellairs,' she said, her tone edged with sharpness.

A slight flush rose to Amanda's cheeks. 'Oh no, of course not. I just mean that if Delcie is ever fortunate enough to live here again she should fill the place with antiques.'

'Didn't you say Richard is already interested in them?' The question came from Brad.

'It's just that I've heard he is, but then I don't know him at all well,' explained Amanda carefully.

'And I haven't yet met him,' Delcie pointed out with some heat. 'Somehow I get the feeling you're trying to marry me off to this man. I can only hope the same feeling doesn't convey itself to him.'

She fell silent as the car stopped at the wide front steps and a tall man came through the open door to greet them. He was followed by a woman of average height whose golden hair had streaks of grey, and who was obviously Richard's mother.

As Amanda had said, Richard Dillon was handsome. His fair hair was sun-bleached and his grey eyes sparkled with interest as they took in Delcie's appearance. But it was his pleasant ease of manner that dispelled the awkwardness of that first meeting as he took her hand and said. 'Well, if it isn't that chubby little three-year-old all grown up.'

'We've met before?' she faltered in a shy voice.

'Of course we've met before, even if you don't remember. At that stage I was ten and not yet into the woman scene. Girls were to be avoided at all costs, no matter how young and innocent.'

Mary Dillon was also intrested in Delcie's appearance. She gazed long and searchingly into her face until at last she said, 'My dear, you're Denise all over again, except that you have your father's eyes. They are not easily forgotten because they were such a beautiful blue.' Her own eyes became suspiciously moist, causing her to dab at them.

Richard said hastily, 'The moment Mother knew you were coming she was here in a flash.'

'Of course I came at once,' Mary said. 'I haven't seen Joan for ages, nor have I met Amanda before today, although I've heard Richard speak of her.' She led them from the hall and into a large lounge furnished by chairs and settees from an earlier period.

Delcie stood staring about her, trying to recapture even the slightest memory, but her mind was blank. She then became aware that the others were darting unobtrusive glances at her, and suddenly she felt like a foolish child who had to be humoured.

Mary Dillon's voice was full of understanding as she said, 'I know you must be longing to look over the house after all the years that have passed since you were here. Come with me and I'll give you a tour of inspection. I'm sure the others will excuse us.' She took Delcie's arm and began to lead her from the room.

Amanda spoke eagerly. 'May I come too?' she pleaded.

Mary looked at her thoughtfully. 'If you wish,' she said.

Delcie was disappointed. She had no desire for Amanda's company while she was being shown through her old home for the first time. In actual fact she longed to wander about the house alone so that she could stand at windows and silently imagine that perhaps her mother had once stood there. However, this was a request that good manners prevented her from making.

Pausing to glance back from the doorway, she was surprised to see the varying expressions on the faces of the people being left in the room. Richard was regarding her in a kindly and compassionate manner, while Joan watched Amanda, a slight frown on her face. As for Brad, there was no doubting the mockery in his eyes, nor the slight smirk about his mouth. *Go upstairs and look at your future bedroom*, he seemed to be saying. It was almost as though he resented her interest in this house; she returned his gaze with a hint of defiance as she left the room.

Mary led them first to the book-lined den which lay across the hall from the lounge. Next she took them to the dining-room with its mahogany table and chairs, and beyond it lay the kitchen, storeroom and laundry. Upstairs they were shown the five bedrooms, and as they stood on the balcony outside the main bedrooom Delcie began to have vague stirrings of having known the place before these moments.

'Was there a swing somewhere?' she asked hesitantly.

'You remember it?' Mary asked eagerly. 'It hung from the bough of a large Australian gumtree but I'm afraid the ropes rotted many years ago. Richard will show you where the tree grows.'

'I love this old furniture,' Amanda remarked wistfully as she ran her hand over the smooth surface of a washstand with its Royal Doulton toilet set of large bowl, water jug and soap dish.

'A few old pieces have always belonged in the house,' Mary said. 'It changed hands four or five times before your father bought it,' she told Delcie. 'When we bought it we tried to furnish it in the style of its period. Within reason, of course,' she added with a smile. 'One must have modern conveniencies and appliances.'

Amanda looked about her. 'Richard keeps the place very well,' she remarked naïvely.

His mother laughed. '*Richard* keeps it well? Surely you don't imagine that he does the housework? He has a married couple living with him, and they take care of the house and garden while he runs the farm. Mrs Collins was probably in their cottage when I showed you the kitchen.'

They went downstairs again and as soon as they entered the lounge the two men stood up.

Mary Dillon looked at her son. 'I'm sure Delcie would like to see the garden and the outside sheds, and particularly where the swing used to hang. You take her while I talk to Joan.'

'Sure,' he agreed amiably, and as he led Delcie from the room Amanda began to accompany them until Brad's voice caused her to pause and look back at him.

'Why don't you leave them to it?' he drawled.

'Because I want to see the place, too,' she flashed at him with a smile that held a hint of defiance.

He did not press the point, and Delcie suspected that Amanda's tactics in trying to make Brad jealous were really succeeding. But at this point she was too interested in her surroundings to give the question much thought.

Richard led them beyond the back yard. He pointed out the old red stables used for draught horses in earlier days, explaining that they had long since been replaced by modern tractors. He showed them the old harness room, the tractor shed and the hay-barn. There was a cat with her kittens, and a row of dog kennels within the shelter of trees.

Delcie saw it all in a dreamlike haze, her imagination revolving about her father who had worked among these sheds and in those distant fields. He, too, had been tall and fair. Had he looked just a little like Richard? she wondered. The thought made her feel drawn towards her host, although not in the same way that she felt drawn to Brad. Right from the start that had been an entirely different stirring of her emotions.

'Mother mentioned the swing,' said Richard. 'It was this way.'

He led them away from the yard and along the side of the house to where an ancient blue gum stood near a gate leading into a field. The tree towered above them, its long strips of peeling bark hanging like twisted ribbons in the high branches, its trunk bared in places to show colourful patches of pink, mauve and grey. Pointing upwards, Richard said, 'It hung from that lower bough. Is it possible you remember it?'

Delcie hesitated. 'I think I do——'

Amanda touched his arm. 'I think she'd like to be left alone. Show me the flower garden.'

Delcie hardly saw them leave her. She gazed about her for a few moments and then, grateful for the solitude, she leaned against the gate and stared unseeingly towards the distant ranges.

What would her life have been like if her parents had lived? Would she have become emotionally involved with Richard, the boy next door? She doubted it. He was nice, but he did not make her pulses race.

Would she have met Brad? It was more than possible, because her parents' friends, the Dillons, were also friendly with the Bellamys. Had it been ordained that she should come back to the Wairarapa? Her aunts had done their best to keep her away from the district, and it had taken one of Wellington's windiest days, plus a stairway, to organise her return. A stairway to her own destiny? No, because there was Amanda. Always there was Amanda.

Brad's voice broke into her musings. Unheard, he had come from behind her and his voice now held a hint of surprise. 'You've been left alone? Where are the others?'

'I think they're looking at the flower garden.'

He leaned against the gate, his sleeve touching her

arm. 'Well, what do you think of it all?' His deep voice put the question quietly while his eyes stared across the fields.

His closeness made her breath quicken. 'It's hard to believe I once lived here, yet the place gives me the strange feeling of having been here before.'

'Play your cards right and you'll be here again,' he commented drily. 'It shouldn't be difficult to spend the rest of your life with Richard. He's a jolly good chap.'

She felt nettled. 'Why are you so sure it's what I want to do?'

'Are you saying you don't like him?'

'Not at all. I think he's charming, but he doesn't bowl me over.' Like someone else I know, she added silently to herself.

'You surprise me,' said Brad. 'I was sure you'd be what's known as a pair of sitters for each other. I thought you'd click at first sight.'

'You were wrong,' she snapped.

'Well, don't say you haven't been given the chance.'

Irritation was beginning to get the better of her. 'You sound as if you're dead keen to be rid of me.'

'Definitely not. But maybe I'm rushing things. Perhaps I'm expecting too much too soon.'

'You certainly are,' she almost hissed. 'I'd be more than grateful if you'd stop expecting *anything*.' She turned away to gaze across the nearby field then said in an altered tone, 'Please don't think I'm lacking in gratitude for having been brought here. I've wondered about the place so many times, and now I've seen it my curiosity has been laid to rest.'

'But what about your yearning to live here again?' he asked softly. 'Hasn't that been niggling at you?'

She turned to face him, her eyes wide with surprise. 'Can't you understand that any yearning I've had has been for my mother and father, rather than for the old home? If I married Richard—if I lived here—I'd begin to feel their presence. I might even begin to imagine the property still belonged to them rather than to Richard.'

'That is utter rubbish,' he snapped. 'You're far too sensible to allow such fancies to rule your mind. In any case, you were much too young to remember them. You must feel that way at the moment because deep down you're all stirred up.'

This, she knew, was true, amd she was unable to find convincing words to deny the accusation.

He went on relentlessly, 'Besides, from the moment you feel Richard's child swelling within you, the past will fade into oblivion. You'll look forward to a new life with a family of your own.'

His words brought a deep flush to her cheeks as she continued to stare at him wordlessly.

'The thought of having babies embarrasses you?' The brown eyes became piercing as they seemed to bore into her mind. 'You do understand that Richard will want sons?'

She pulled herself together, then snapped a reply. 'You speak as though it's all cut and dried, but you're forgetting one salient point——'

'And what would that be?' he drawled.

'That it's manners to wait till I'm asked,' she retorted icily.

'Oh, *that*. Just give him time.' His grin was full of confidence. 'You'll meet him again at the party. Mother took care to invite him while you were upstairs.' He raised one brow in a teasing question. 'I presume there's a nice big double bed in the master bedroom?'

'*Shut up!*' she snapped furiously.

Brad grinned again then went on, 'He's definitely keen to come, and there's something else—he admitted he thinks you're one of the prettiest girls he's ever seen. So there you are.'

'Is that a fact?' Her voice was low, the compliment giving her no pleasure at all. Instead she felt despondent as facts of a different nature seeped into her mind, depressing her almost beyond endurance. No man who had any thoughts of love for her would push her towards someone else in this manner, she decided. It seemed to be definite proof that Brad had no real feeling for her at all. No, none at all. No doubt he was being kind, but she didn't want his kindness. She wanted his love, and she knew that now without a shadow of doubt.

The thought made her feel desperate, forcing her to turn upon him with an air of defiance. Her voice still low, she challenged, 'Who are you to talk about sons? What are you doing about raising a family? It makes me laugh to hear you worry about Richard raising one. What about your own, huh? You know perfectly well you'll need sons to inherit your property.'

He gave an easy laugh. 'Never mind about my sons. They'll come all in good time.'

'Really?' Her tone became scathing as she was goaded to ask, 'Exactly how long do you expect Amanda to wait for you?'

'We're getting away from the subject,' he snapped crisply. 'You're the one who concerns me. Can't you understand that I want to see the best happen for you?'

'How kind—how *very* kind. Why is that, may I ask?'

He frowned thougthfully. 'Because—well, because I've taken quite a fancy towards you, I suppose.'

'A *fancy*?' Huh!' She gave a derisive laugh which also held a sting of bitterness.

'I'm telling you, Richard's a jolly fine fellow——'

She turned upon him, her blue eyes flashing with anger. 'Will you please stop pushing me towards Richard.'

He sent her a look of understanding. 'You're becoming upset. Obviously you're in need of a cup of tea. Actually

I'd been sent to out to find everyone because the afternoon tea trolley has been wheeled into the lounge.' He looked about him.

She took a quick dab at her eyes. 'I told you before, they're at the front of the house looking at the flower garden.'

'Then let's find them.'

He led her along a path towards the corner of the house and as they turned it they were given a view of Richard and Amanda standing on the opposite side of the garden. Richard's arm was about her shoulders, his head close to hers as he pointed upwards.

The intimacy of their attitude caused Brad to stand still while he observed them, and even as Delcie glanced at his face to catch his reaction the notes of a bird floated on the air in a long series of sweet double notes which rose in volume before slurring down to end in a chirrup. Then came a flutter of wings as the small feathered creature left the tree.

As Amanda turned to follow its flight across the lawn she called to Brad. 'Did you see it? It was a shining cuckoo. I've never been so close to one,' she exclaimed, her voice animated, her colour slightly higher than usual. 'It was a lovely golden green tinged with copper, its underparts buff with dark bars across it.'

They're wonderful little birds,' Richard said to Delcie. 'I suppose they're seldom heard in the city. It's hard to believe they spend the winter on the Solomon Islands, two thousand miles away, then fly all the way back to New Zealand for our summer months.'

'They lay their eggs in the nest of the grey warblers,' Brad put in with a laugh. 'What a cheek they have.'

Amanda began chatting volubly. 'Richard's been telling me all about the warblers' eggs being kicked out of the nest by the parasite cuckoo.' She sent Delcie a direct glare. 'I think some people can be parasites, too. They step in and take root in places that belong to others.'

Delcie was so taken aback by the veiled attack that she was unable to find a reply, and it was a relief when Brad informed them that tea was being poured in the lounge. She also thought she detected a hint of amusement in his voice, and she wondered if this was meant to inform Amanda that her intimate attitude while watching the cuckoo with Richard hadn't moved him in the least.

They returned to the lounge where they found the two older women chatting amicably, and it needed little for Delcie to guess that she had been the main topic of their conversation.

Mary Dillon looked at her kindly. 'You must come and see us again, my dear. Richard will take you out to see the farm. I'm sure he'd be very pleased to do that.'

Amanda was quick to make an offer. 'I'll drive her here.'

Joan's brows rose as she regarded Amanda. 'Have you forgotten that Delcie has her own car? She can drive herself quite easily.'

'It's just in case she becomes lost,' Amanda explained with the merest pout to her lips.

'That would be most unlikely.' Brad's mouth held a sardonic twist. 'In any case, she won't have much time during the next month.'

'Oh yes, I suppose you'll need her help,' said Mary. 'Such a pity about your hand. When will the plaster come off?'

He hesitated, then admitted casually, 'Oh, possibly any day now. I'm thoroughly fed up with it.'

His mother was shocked. 'Don't be foolish, Brad. It mustn't come off a moment before necessary,'

He gave a short laugh. 'At present I'm managing quite well with one hand, Mother, but the moment I need two, off will come the plaster.'

As he uttered the words Delcie had a sudden vision of

him in the motel at Otaki. The light had been shining
from behind his head. his face had been shadowed while
his whole body had oozed an aura of masculinity. *When I
make love I like to have both hands free*, he had said.

Why on earth should she recall those few moments?
Unwillingly her gaze was drawn towards him, almost as
though her head was being turned by a giant magnet, and
she was not surprised to find him regarding her, because
she had definitely felt the drawing power of his
penetrating brown eyes.

When he spoke his tone was firm. 'It's time we were
going home.'

Going home. The words had a lovely ring about them,
she thought wistfully—then recalled they had been on
her mind during the drive out to this place. She had felt
she was going home then, too, but she now knew that it
was a return to Bellairs that meant going home.

As they walked out to the car Mary took Delcie's arm
in a friendly manner. 'You probably know that this is
Richard's place,' she said, 'but his father and I live
further along the road. Ours is the next entrance on the
left. Derek, my husband, has always been keen on
photography, and if you visit us it's possible I could find
some snapshots which include your parents.'

Delcie's eyes shone. 'You *could*? You really have
photos of my mother and father?'

'I'd have to search through a number of old boxes
because it's over twenty years since they were taken,'
Mary reminded her.

'I can remember when Derek became interested in
home movies,' said Joan. 'Is he still keen on them?'

Mary smiled. 'No. I'm afraid television has replaced
his home movies although he still has several of his old
reels. Actually I wasn't going to mention them until I'd
made sure Delcie's parents were on some of the ones he's
kept.'

'Are you saying he's destroyed some of his home movies?' Delcie asked, her hopes sinking at once.

'Some of his early attempts were discarded because he became dissatisfied with them,' Mary explained. 'I remember that some were taken when he went with Denise and Ray for a picnic along a stream closer to the ranges. There was a bush that shut out the sun, so of course the pictures were rather dark. But he was still experimenting with his camera in those days. However, if they've gone I'm afraid it can't be helped.'

Delcie nodded, forcing herself to smile. 'I'll understand.' But within herself she felt sure that anything featuring her parents would have been destroyed.

Amanda who had been listening to the conversation, said quickly, 'Mr Dillon is sure to have kept that particular reel. I'd love to see them, too.' She looked at Mary hopefully, waiting for an invitation.

But Mary remained silent until she spoke to Delcie again. 'I'll phone you after I've searched through all our old snapshots, and after Derek has looked at his earlier movies,' she promised.

'Thank you, you're very kind,' said Delcie gratefully.

'And you're a very sweet girl,' Mary smiled as she placed an impulsive kiss on Delcie's cheek.

As they drove away Joan looked over her shoulder to speak to Delcie. 'Well, my dear,' she said with undisguised satisfaction, 'you certainly made a conquest there. It's obvious that Mary loved you on sight. I could tell she'd welcome you with open arms as a daughter-in-law.'

The words made Delcie feel slightly hysterical, but she controlled herself and said, 'I'm sure she'd be a most understanding mother-in-law, but only if I happened to be Richard's choice. Don't you think so, Amanda?' She turned to the girl sitting beside her.

But Amanda's dark eyes held only an angry glitter.

'She didn't invite me,' she said belligerently. 'I hinted loudly enough—I *told* her I'd like to see the home movies too, but did she ask me to come with you? No, she did not.' She glared at Delcie without making any attempt to disguise her extreme disappointment.

'I can't imagine that they'd be of the slightest interest to you,' Brad drawled from across his shoulder.

'You don't really know what interests me,' Amanda snapped. 'You're either locked in your office or away out on the farm giving orders to staff.'

'Now then, Mandy,' Joan cut in. 'We've had a happy day, so please don't spoil it by becoming upset over a trifle.'

'It is not a trifle,' Amanda retorted, then lapsed into a sulky silence which made the atmosphere uncomfortable.

Her attitude puzzled Delcie, and she could not understand why Amanda considered it so important that she should be invited to view the home movies. She also knew that Brad was observing the dark-haired girl in the rear view mirror, but although his eyes held a question, he made no comment.

Amanda did not speak again until they were nearing the end of the hilly country, when she surprised them by leaning forward to tap Brad on the shoulder. 'Would you please stop the car on the sharp bend at the top of the last hill. There's a low white rail edging the road.'

His frown was reflected in the mirror. 'Stop the car? What on earth for?'

'I just want to look at something,' she replied without further elucidation.

'Something—like what?' he demanded.

'Stop the car at the top of the last hill,' was all she said.

They reached the summit where the road curved round the high contour before twisting down to the lower levels of the plains. Brad stopped the car on the grassy verge beside the low white railings, and as he pulled on the brake Amanda leaned across Delcie to stare down the bank on their left.

It was a long steep slope, broken by gullies and strewn by jagged outcrops of limestone. It was a place where a rolling car would not be brought to a halt, and as Delcie's eyes followed the direction of Amanda's gaze she was gripped by a sudden cold horror that sent spasms of fear shivering down her spine. She almost felt the blood drain from her face as, cringing against the back of the seat, she was unable to control a cry that echoed terror.

'*It was there*, wasn't it?' she croaked hoarsely. 'That's where we went over the bank—that's where my mother and father were killed. *You wanted me to see the place*——' Her voice rose with hysteria as she became shaken by a storm of weeping.

Joan twisted in her seat to face Amanda. 'Is that true? Is this the place?' She was looking at Amanda incredulously.

'Yes. Richard told me they went over the top of the last hill. The railing was put there later——'

Brad's voice exploded with barely controlled fury. 'Damn it, Amanda, that was unkind. You're a bitch!'

'I am not,' she defended hotly. 'Sooner or later she'd learn where it happened, especially if she's going to be driving back and forth to visit the Dillons,' she added with bitter sarcasm.

'But why tell her *now*?' Joan's face held a shocked expression, almost as though she was seeing Amanda for the first time. 'Was it a deliberate attempt to upset Delcie?'

'It's because she's mad with me,' Delcie explained wearily, her eyes brimming with tears that made them look like mid-ocean depths. 'She's furious because Mrs Dillon didn't invite her to see the home movies. But she's right when she says that sooner or later I'd want to know where it happened.'

'Right? Of course I'm right.' Amanda's voice echoed triumph. 'And now that you know your mind should be free of all morbid questions. I've really done you a good turn.'

Brad turned on the ignition and the car glided down the hill, the silence in it becoming tense.

Delcie remained huddled against the back of the seat, her eyes closed. But instead of shutting out the sight of the steep slope with its craggy outcrops the scene became intensified until suddenly her body was convulsed by a long shudder that rose from within the depths of her mind.

Brad's voice grated harshly across his shoulder. 'Snap out of it, Delcie. You're wallowing in self-pity.'

She sat upright to glare at the brown eyes regarding her in the rear view mirror. 'I am not. *How dare you*——'

'Now who's being unkind?' Amanda hit back at Brad for his previous remark to herself.

Joan became exasperated. '*Please*, everybody, can't we let this matter drop?' Then, as though defending her son, she turned to stare at Amanda, a pained expression on her face. 'As Brad said, you were most unkind, and I must say I'm surprised and very disappointed to know you'd deliberately hurt Delcie in this manner. No doubt she'd have learnt of the place soon enough, but I can't see that there was any need to point it out today.'

Amanda made no reply, her casual shrug clearly indicating she couldn't care less about Joan's opinion of her actions, and for the rest of the journey she stared through the window in sulky silence.

Delcie was puzzled by her attitude which seemed to be so far removed from the closeness of her friendship with Joan, and she was even further surprised when, on reaching home, Amanda got into her car and drove away with hardly a word to anyone.

Her departure made Delcie feel unhappy because she knew that she herself lay at the root of the rift that had suddenly opened between them, and although neither Joan nor Brad remarked upon Amanda's absence at the dinner table, the empty chair did nothing to alleviate Delcie's feeling of guilt.

She did her best to do justice to the delicious chicken Maryland wheeled into the dining-room by Sally, but she was thankful when the meal ended. Then, murmuring her excuses, she made her way to the office where she began working on a pile of pages Brad had left ready to be typed. Work was her greatest need, she realised. It was the only way in which to wipe all thoughts of that hillside from her mind.

CHAPTER EIGHT

DELCIE had not been mistaken about the value of work and concentration. Nor was it long before visions of the hillside and the memory of Amanda's sullen mood faded into the background. She even reached the stage where, as her spirits rose, gurgles of mirth escaped her as she recorded the antics of a small French poodle that did its best to tell its owner the phone was ringing.

Engrossed, she did not hear Brad enter the room, nor was she aware of his presence until he came from behind to bend and rest his cheek against her own. At the same time his hands slid round her body to cup each breast.

The shock of his action was superseded by the shock of looking down to see two hands. 'You've removed the plaster!' she gasped.

'Yes. My fingers seem to be OK.' He moved the digits of both hands, running them gently over her nipples that leapt to become erect rosebuds as they responded to his touch. Her sharp intake of breath betrayed agitation as she endeavoured to remove his hands. 'Brad, please—— Are you sure it's all right to remove the plaster?'

He examined his hand reflectively, bending the fingers one by one. 'I don't believe there was much damage done, at least not as much as was at first thought.'

'But—but the X-ray must have shown damage?'

'I wasn't given a view of it. I was simply told that plaster would give the fingers a chance to get over the shock of having had a ton weight land on them.'

She became conscious of a rising suspicion. 'I suppose you really did need the plaster? It wasn't just a ploy——?'

'A ploy? To what end?' A glitter of amusement appeared in his eyes as he awaited her answer.

But already she was regretting her words and was

unable to voice the question running through her mind.

He did it for her. 'Are you suggesting I had the plaster put on as a ploy to enlist your assistance?'

She felt contrite. 'To be honest I did wonder about it, but for only a moment, because at that stage you were unaware that I could give the kind of assistance you needed. Besides, one can't dictate to the people running hospital departments. If they decided plaster was necessary, then no doubt it was essential.'

'And the pain I suffered at the time? You're sure you don't think that was just put on?'

'No—no of course not.' She was appalled by the suggestion, especially when she recalled the white tightness of his face as she had driven him to the hospital. 'I'm sorry I used the word ploy. I didn't mean it.'

'Is that supposed to be an apology?'

'What else can I say?' She looked up at him helplessly.

'I'd rather be given satisfaction in a more pleasant manner. Like this, for instance——' His strong left hand seized her arm and drew her from the typing chair to a standing position. Then, turning her to face him, he enfolded her in his arms.

His right hand minus its plaster fingered the strands of her blonde hair, twining tendrils into curls as his lips followed a diagonal line from her brow to her mouth, and as his hand slid the length of her form, possessively pressing her against his body, she was made aware of how restricted his previous embraces had been.

The aura of his masculinity flooded over her, seeping into every part of her being and wafting her into a mindless state until, at the end of that kiss, she opened her eyes to gaze up at him.

The face that stared back at her was completely expressionless, dragging her spirits down from the clouds with sudden force, and as her feet touched earth she was jerked into the realisation that he was studying her with a cool, almost speculative manner.

'Is something wrong?' she ventured.

'No, except that I don't know what to do about you.'

She was nonplussed. 'Why should you have to do anything about me? Really, I don't understand.'

'I'll admit things didn't turn out as I expected.'

'You really thought I'd fall into Richard's arms? I'm sorry if you're disappointed.'

'Doesn't the opportunity to live in your old home again appeal to you?' He was watching her intently.

She turned incredulous eyes upon him. 'Surely you don't imagine I'd marry Richard just for the sake of living in my old home?'

'There are some of whom it could be possible.'

'How little you know me,' she snapped angrily, then her glance softened. 'Still, I appreciate that you meant well because you thought it would be to my benefit, whereas your mother and Amanda——' She paused, then fell silent.

'Yes? What about Mother and Amanda? Explain yourself, blue eyes,' he demanded crisply.

'It was they who arranged to take me to meet Richard today,' she reminded him. 'And one doesn't have to be the world's greatest clairvoyant to guess why.'

'Wasn't it to show you your old home?'

'I think there was more to it than that. So, if everyone has expected me to fall into Richard's arms I'm afraid they're to be disappointed,' she finished heatedly.

'Amanda wasn't disappointed,' he said softly.

She blinked at him. 'What do you mean?'

He chuckled. 'Little one, I'm beginning to wonder if you're as bright as I thought you were. Perhaps you'd better come closer and let me explain.'

He drew her against him again, but although she longed to cling to him, and to respond by lifting her face for his kisses, she had a sudden horror of Joan Bellamy entering the room to discover them in each other's arms.

The thought was enough to send tremors of agitation racing through her nerves. 'Brad stop it. Your mother might come in,' she gasped.

'So what?' he demanded nonchalantly.

'You can ask so what? According to her you belong to Amanda—*that's* what.'

He frowned. 'It really worries you?'

'Of course it does. I can't concentrate. I make typing errors. I can't work with her wrath hovering over my head.' And finding the strength to struggle from his arms she fled upstairs to the haven of her bedroom.

A short time later she was making an effort to get Brad out of her mind. Propped up in bed she sat reading a book, but it was one he had written and, as her eyes skimmed the lines, his flow of words, his turn of phrase, even his personality rose up from the pages to engulf her in spasms of intense longing.

They brought back the memory of his arms holding her closely, the pressure of his lips on her own. Then some of his words floated into her mind, words that puzzled her. What had he meant when he had said she was not as bright as he'd thought her to be? In what way was she being mentally dull? She put the book aside, switched off the light and lay down to think about it.

Was it because she had failed to show more than a casual interest in the present owner of her old home? Admittedly Richard had a ready smile and a pleasant personality, but she didn't hear bells ringing when she thought about him.

As for the house, the first peep when approaching it would not be the same one offered so long ago to her parents. Since their time the trees had attained twenty or more years' growth, while the garden had to be more developed. And even if the house was structurally the same, the inside decorations and furniture must be totally different. Nor did the odd piece of antique crockery that had been there during earlier years do anything to wipe away the intervening period of time.

No, her old home had gone. It had held a dreamtime place in her mind and the sooner she got rid of it the better. Still, it was nice to have seen the house, and for

this she had Joan and Amanda to thank. And through
them she had met Mary Dillon whose husband had taken
home movies that might enable her to see her parents—
that's if he hadn't discarded the reel. Bemused, she felt
the darkness crowding in about her. Her lids fluttered
and she slept.

Next morning dawned with the warmth and perfec-
tion of a summer day that sent Delcie springing from her
bed. She showered and dressed in a lilac sundress she had
not previously worn, and as she brushed her blonde hair
she gazed through the window to where a line of tall
poplars stood silhouetted against the blue sky. Sheep
grazed beneath them, giving an atmosphere of peace, yet
there was turmoil in her own mind.

And this, she realised, was stirred by thoughts of Brad
and the memory of his caresses. She was also acutely
aware that her own response to him was becoming more
intense, more uninhibited, and, loving him as she did,
she feared that her control might snap.

He had now kissed her on several occasions, she
recalled, and the burning question nagging at her mind
was, *why*? And while at first she had thought it had been
a means of persuasion to keep her happily at the
typewriter, that reason was now brushed aside because
he knew she had promised to see the manuscript
finished.

She didn't believe he was in love with her, either. If he
loved her as she loved him, she would have seen a sign of
it—wouldn't she? She would have noticed something
very different from knowing herself being shoved
towards another man like Richard Dillon.

So did his kisses merely mean he was being patient
while awaiting the opportunity to satisfy his male needs?
And the plaster was off his hand now. He preferred to
have both hands free when he made love—he had told
her so. At the time she hadn't thought a great deal about
the statement, but now she wondered if she should look
upon it as a warning.

When she went downstairs she met Sally's mother in the hall. 'Oh, there you are,' the housekeeper said. 'I've just taken Mrs Bellamy's breakfast up to her, and as Brad has gone out I wondered if you'd like to have yours in the kitchen with Sally and me.' The grey eyes looked at her kindly as she added, 'There's no need for you so sit alone in that big dining-room.'

'Mrs Bellamy is all right?' Delcie asked anxiously. 'It's unusual for her to remain in bed.'

Olga Brown led the way to the kitchen. 'She came down earlier in her dressing-gown. I thought she looked so tired I persuaded her to go back to bed. She admitted she hadn't slept well and would be glad of a few hours of extra rest.'

A short time later Delcie sat at the kitchen table with a plate of scrambled eggs before her. She had seen very little of Olga's domain, and as she looked about her she realised the kitchen held almost every home appliance on the market.

Olga said casually, 'I noticed that Amanda didn't stay for dinner last night. Most unusual for her, don't you think?'

Delcie realised that a reply was expected, but as she had no wish to discuss Amanda she feigned innocence. 'Is it? I wouldn't know,' was all she said.

Olga sent her a shrewd look. 'Surely you've been in this house long enough to see that she almost lives here, except for this last week when she's hardly set foot in the place—which is another thing that's mighty strange, to my way of thinking.'

'Yes, I suppose it is.'

'I can't help feeling there's been—*something*—that's upset Mrs Bellamy.' Olga's tone held a question.

Delcie met the grey eyes steadily. She knew the housekeeper had Joan's interest at heart, and she also knew it was not her place to discuss the matter, so she said carefully, 'If Brad's mother is upset she didn't tell me about it. Did you say he has gone away somewhere?'

Sally poured three cups of coffee. 'He hasn't gone further then the big hill where he's working with Wag, his huntaway. I suppose you know what a huntaway is?'

Delcie laughed. 'After all that typing about sheepdogs you can be sure I know that—a huntaway is one that barks whereas a heading dog runs out and silently heads the sheep in the direction indicated by the boss's whistles.'

'The way they work is quite wonderful,' said Olga.

Delcie looked at her thoughtfully. It was almost as though Olga welcomed the change of subject. Does she fear I might guess I'd been invited into the kitchen simply to be questioned? she wondered.

Sally said, 'The big hill is fairly long and steep. Two sets of markers have been placed on it and Wag is being trained to drive three sheep through them to a gate at the top. If you'd like to watch just follow the sound of barking and whistles.'

Delcie thought about it, then shook her head. 'No, I think I'll go to the office and get on with the job.'

A protest came from Olga. 'But it's Sunday and a beautiful morning. I'm sure he'd like you to see Wag at work,' she urged. 'Let him see you can show more interest than Amanda.'

'But I thought Amanda showed tremendous interest in him.'

The housekeeper's tone became blunt. 'Amanda's interest lies mainly in herself, but apart from that her interest in anything else is mainly superficial, whereas you——'

Delcie was amazed by the way the conversation had twisted. Her blue eyes were full of questions as she said, 'Yes? Me?'

'Well, there's more depth to your character. You'd be a much better match for Brad Bellamy.'

'You're being very frank, Mrs Brown.'

The older woman smiled. 'I'm noted for my frankness. I know I'm only the housekeeper, but I say what I think.

And while the kitchen is my domain I'm not blind to what goes on in the rest of the house. And, believe it or not, there have been times when my advice has been asked for,' she added with quiet satisfaction.

Delcie looked at the homely face that had common sense written all over it. 'That doesn't surprise me, Mrs Brown. So, what would be your advice to me?'

'I'd go right out there and let him see you in that pretty lilac dress. I'd let him see the sun shining on that lovely blonde hair. I wish I had a slight wave and ends that curled up so nicely,' she added as though sighing for youth that was no longer with her.

Delcie let the compliment pass as she said, 'It's possible Brad doesn't want to be disturbed.'

'Nonsense,' Olga retorted briskly. 'He's been out there for ages. Heaven alone knows how many times Wag has sent sheep up the hill. Now you go and watch.'

A short time later they directed Delcie towards a track lying beyond the back yard. It led past sheds and round the foot of a steep face to where Brad stood beside an enclosure containing a few sheep. Half-way up the hill a large black and tan sheepdog barked loudly as he endeavoured to drive three sheep in a straight line up the slope. Whistles from Brad not only told him when to bark, but also steered his movements right and left as the sheep approached the white stakes marking the course.

Delcie was fascinated as she stood watching the performance from a short distance. She knew that Brad sent her a brief glance, but apart from that he ignored her.

At last the sheep disappeared through the open gate at the top of the hill while Wag, tail aloft, looked down at his master with a satisfied air. Further whistles then brought him back to base where three more sheep were released to be sent up the hill.

Delcie continued to stand still, being undecided about what she should do. Would she distract Wag if she approached and stood beside Brad? She doubted it but felt she should wait for a beckoning sign from him. However, none came.

Disappointed, she remained where she was, watching Wag's efforts and listening to the whistles and barks that rang on the still morning air while scraps of conversation from the kitchen returned to her mind. *Let him see the sun shining on your lovely blonde hair*, Olga Brown had said. Huh! She could be bald for all he cared, she thought bitterly. *Let him see you in that pretty lilac dress*—huh! If she stood in the nude his eyes wouldn't shift from that hillside. And if he loved her just the tiniest scrap he would have beckoned her to come and stand beside him. Sadly, she turned and walked back to the house.

It was a relief to find her way to the solitude of the office which was fast becoming a place of refuge for her mind. It was a haven where unhappy thoughts could be wiped away while she worked at the typewriter, the latest thought being the knowledge that she held no special interest for the man she loved. Hadn't she just played second fiddle to a dog?

Irritation sent an unnecessary force into her fingers, but a short time later this subsided abruptly when Brad's voice spoke from behind her. He had come into the room unheard and now stood looking at her with amused toleration.

'Is it necessary to hammer that machine on the Sabbath?' he asked in a drawl she was beginning to know.

She shrugged. 'Just as necessary as it is to make the welkin ring with whistles and barks.'

He regarded her closely. 'I see. Cross, this morning, are we? And just as we're looking so nice in our lilac dress. I think we've been working too hard. A run in the country is called for.'

Surprised, she turned to stare at him. 'A run in the country?'

'I thought I'd take you for a drive to the Mount Bruce Native Bird Reserve. We'll leave after lunch.'

'Oh, that'll be nice. I've never been there.' His words had lifted her spirits, completely disarming her, and for the rest of the morning she was conscious of a simmering excitement caused by the anticipation of going out with Brad.

They left soon after the midday meal and as the Renault covered the fifteen miles between Masterton and the reserve he told her a little about the purpose of the place. 'It's really designed to preserve specimens of our rare native birds in what is the most natural bush environment for them,' he explained. 'Their breeding habits are studied and encouraged, and when possible some are liberated in areas suitable for their particular species.'

She listened happily, enjoying the timbre of his deep voice while he told her about the pukeko, the kakapo and the kiwi—the native pigeon, parrakeet and saddle-back. But at heart she knew she couldn't have cared less if the reserve had been breeding rats instead of birds. Brad was taking her out and at the moment her cup was full.

When they arrived at the bush area with its large cages he led her to a particular enclosure and said, 'There it is—the takahe—thought to be extinct for fifty years until a small colony was discovered near Lake Te Anau in the South Island.'

She examined the heavy flightless bird with its pink bill and legs, its indigo throat, breast and thighs and its metallic olive-green back. 'I had no idea its colours were so lovely,' she said. Then, gazing about her. 'In fact everything is lovely. The bush is beautiful and that pond with so many ducks looks so peaceful.'

He looked at her intently. 'You've really enjoyed coming here?'

Her eyes shone as she looked up at him. 'Oh yes, I've loved it. Thank you for bringing me.' And then her contentment deepened as she felt his fingers entwined about her own.

He led her from one cage to another where they

examined every bird in the enclosures, and as they wandered leisurely along the secluded bush tracks she longed for him to take her in his arms. To be kissed in this place would be unforgettable, but to be told he loved her would make it just perfect.

But of course nothing of the sort happened. Instead he glanced hurriedly at his watch and said, 'By Jove, it's nearly two-thirty. We'd better get moving.' And, taking her arm, he almost ran her back to the car.

She was puzzled by his haste, and even more surprised when he roared the motor and headed north instead of turning back towards Masterton. 'Where are we going?' she ventured.

'To see a man about a dog,' he grinned.

Her jaw dropped slightly. 'You're going to interview someone?'

'Yes. The tape recorder is under the rug on the back seat. There's a man whose golden Labrador is the most intelligent dog in the world—or so he says. He wants me to see him in action.'

'So this is where we were heading all the time?'

'Yes, you could say so. I thought we could call in at Mount Bruce on the way.'

She stared straight ahead as she fought down bitter disappointment. What an utter fool she'd been to have thought he was taking her out. What an idiot to have imagined even for one moment that he had wanted her company.

'Is something the matter?' he asked quietly.

'What makes you think so?' she hedged.

He sent her a side glance. 'I can sense it. You've gone all silent. In the bush you were like a ray of sunshine but now the clouds have descended and you look depressed.'

She shook herself mentally. Lord, was she so very transparent? Yet she remained lost for words.

'I'm still waiting for an answer,' he persisted. 'What's bugging you? I don't like people who blow hot one minute and cold the next.'

'And I don't like people who say they're taking me out when they're not doing anything of the sort,' she retorted, her pride slipping away from her. 'It gives me one of those horrible—let down feelings.'

He kept his eyes on the road ahead. 'I see. Well, please believe me when I say I wanted you to come. If not, I'd have come alone. It's as simple as that.'

This, she realised was true, and the thought cheered her sufficiently to ask questions about the Labrador they were going to see.

'His name's Jake,' Brad said. 'His owner can lay out a row of tools and Jake will fetch whichever one is asked for. When the boss chops firewood Jake will carry it piece by piece to the woodbox. He'll even collect the eggs without breaking or eating one, and I'm told he can open and shut gates.'

'He sounds terrific.' Delcie smiled, trying to feel cheerful.

'He is. And what's more his owner has photos of him busy with his activities, so they'll be a help with the illustrations.'

'Yes, a great help,' she agreed absently, her thoughts not really on Jake or his activities, but on the remark Brad had made previously. *Believe me when I say I wanted you to come*, he had said.

At the time the words had made her feel happier, but now she began to look at them from a different angle. Of course he wanted her to come. He needed her to carry and handle the tape recorder, especially if they were outside with Jake and his owner. The plaster might have been removed from his hand, but he was still giving it as little use as possible, so once again it was her assistance rather than her company that he needed. Blast the man, and blast her own stupidity in allowing herself to reach the stage of longing for more than he was prepared to give.

It was late afternoon when they arrived home to find Joan busily writing invitations to the coming Christmas party. Delcie had expected to find Amanda with her, but the dark-haired girl was conspicuous only by her absence.

This was also noted by Brad, who looked at the pile of addressed envelopes. 'I thought Amanda was supposed to help you with these invitations,' he remarked idly.

Joan made no attempt to diguise her irritation. 'So did I. I phoned and told her I was doing them, and I also asked her to come for the evening meal, but when I told her you'd taken Delcie for an outing she found excuses.'

'Don't let it worry you, Mother,' Brad said lightly. 'Everything will be OK.'

'But it *does* worry me,' she snapped crossly, then turned reproachful eyes upon Delcie as though wordlessly adding that the entire reason for Amanda's absence lay at her feet. 'I hope you enjoyed your outing,' she said pointedly.

'Yes, thank you,' Delcie assured her sweetly. 'I loved seeing the native birds—and Jake was amazing.'

Joan's brows rose. '*Jake?*'

'A golden Labrador. The outing was really just another interview. The birds happened to be on the route.'

'Oh, I didn't know.' She looked perplexed.

Brad spoke to his mother, his voice gritting with impatience. 'Don't you think it's time you stopped moaning for Amanda? I've told you that everything will be all right.'

Delcie made a hasty departure towards the office, mainly because she had no wish to hear what might burst forth in a mother-son discussion about relationships with Amanda. But at the same time Brad's words had sent spasms of fear through her. Surely they could only mean that everything his mother had wished for was about to come to pass—that he and Amanda——

She pushed the thought from her, clearing her mind of depression by finishing the page already in the typewriter, and it was as she reached towards the pile of fresh sheets that she happened to glance at the calendar hanging on the wall. The date startled her, sending her thoughts racing towards Christmas shopping. Gifts for the aunts must be purchased and then posted to them.

Next morning she mentioned this fact to Brad while they sat at breakfast. 'It means I must spend a few hours in Masterton,' she explained, half apologetically.

'That's OK, take the day off,' he said easily. 'If you need money there's some deposited in your name in the Bank of New Zealand.'

She laughed. 'You mean in Wellington. I don't have an account in Masterton.'

'You have now. I opened one for you last week. Do you think my pride would allow you to do all this work for nothing?'

She went scarlet. 'But I don't expect money for something I do so quickly and easily. Besides, have you forgotten that it was I who caused the accident?'

'Forgotten? How could I forget? Nevertheless, I would have to pay somebody to do the work, and it's nice to see the job being done by an expert.' He paused, then added by way of changing the subject which appeared to be embarrassing her, 'It's possible I might see you in Masterton. I have a little business to do there this afternoon.'

Later, as she browsed in the Masterton shopping area, she avoided the bank. The thought of the money lodged on her behalf made her feel uncomfortable, and she didn't need it anyway because she had her own cheque book. However, before she made any purchases she decided to examine the long line of shops on either side of the main street that ran through the centre of the town.

Gifts for the aunts did not present problems that were too great. She knew that Aunt Lois always preferred something practical like a box of good quality writing paper, while Aunt Alice loved pure silk scarves which could be tied to hide the lines in her neck.

A gift for Joan caused a little more thought until she saw a bottle of her own favourite *Oscar de la Renta*

perfume, and in the same shop she found special bath
soap for Amanda. She feared that a gift from herself
could possibly be that last thing Amanda would
appreciate, but not for one moment would Delcie leave
her off the list.

Gifts for Sally and her mother were also purchased,
and then she faced the greatest problem of all: Brad.
What did one buy for this man who already had
everything he needed? Anthing she gave him would be a
mere duplication of something he already had, so the
ideal gift would be something that might—just *might*—
remind him him of herself. A glance at her watch told her
it was after one o'clock. Perhaps lunch would help her to
think about it.

She found her way to a restaurant where the tables
were partly concealed from each other by dividing walls
which formed small open-ended cubicles. The place was
full of people and she had to carry her tray with its tea
and asparagus rolls to the last table at the end of the
room.

The table was in a shadowed area, and as she sipped
her tea she watched people enter or leave the various
cubicles—and all the time the question of gift for Brad
continued to revolve in her mind. It must be something
personal, she decided, but what personal item could
possibly remind him of her?

She thought of his hand now without its plaster, and
then inspiration flashed. *Cufflinks*. Gold cufflinks with a
dog's head engraved on one link and his initials on the
other. Would they remind him of her—just a little? She
even knew his initials were B.A.B. for Brad Antony
Bellamy because she had seen his full name on a share
certificate envelope.

She was so pleased with her idea that she failed to
notice the couple who entered the end cubicle across the
aisle until the girl's ringing voice came to her ears.

'Darling, I'm sorry to be so late.'

The voice was familiar enough to make Delcie's

thoughts freeze, but, turning her head slowly, she was amazed to see Amanda and Richard Dillon settling themselves at the opposite table.

They were completely engrossed in each other, she realised, as, fascinated, she watched while he leaned forward to plant a swift kiss on Amanda's mouth, then lifted her hands to brush his lips across her fingers. Amanda's eyes glowed as she gazed at him, the whole scene speaking for itself.

It was several minutes before they became aware of Delcie's presence. It occurred when Richard happened to glance across the aisle and as he did so their eyes met. His manner was at once jovial. 'Hi, there. If it isn't little Delcie.'

Amanda turned to follow his gaze. Her jaw dropped slightly and she appeared to be struck dumb. Her face went scarlet, a fact which made Delcie want to laugh. It was the first time that she, personally, had had Amanda at a disadvantage.

CHAPTER NINE

AMANDA was quick to regain her composure. She looked at the gift-wrapped parcels on Delcie's table and said. 'You're in town for Christmas shopping? Brad isn't with you?'

'If he is he's invisible,' Delcie returned lightly. 'However, he did say he'd be in town to do some business.'

Amanda smiled sweetly. 'Please remember me to him.'

'I'll do that.' Delcie smiled in return, then poured herself a second cup of tea. From the corner of her eye she saw Amanda shrug before turning away to give her full attenion to Richard.

When Delcie left the restaurant she made her way to a large jewellery shop she had noticed in the town. The windows gleamed with an array of diamond rings that caught and held her gaze, although she knew it was useless to give them as much as a second glance because nobody was likely to place one on her finger.

A sigh escaped her as she entered the shop, and when she explained what she had in mind to an assistant he led her to a glass topped case filled with cufflinks of all descriptions.

'We have just what you need,' he said. 'Some of these are nine carat gold presentation sets. We have them engraved with horse heads for racing enthusiasts, or with trout for anglers. Here we have a set with border collie heads for dog trialists. The second link is left bare for initials. Our engraver could have a pair initialled by three-thirty this afternoon.'

It was a relief to have Brad's Christmas present solved and she then went to the post office to dispatch the presents she had bought for the aunts. She lingered for a while, buying stamps for herself, and it was as she was leaving the post office that she saw Brad's tall figure in the distance.

He walked rapidly, purpose in every stride, and as she hastened to catch up with him she saw him enter the jeweller's shop. She stopped, hesitating, and was suddenly assailed by the memory of Amanda's petulance after spending a day in town with him. She had been annoyed, Delcie recalled, because Brad had refused to take her into the jeweller's shop.

Had Amanda thought he had been about to buy her an engagement ring? If so, it would be something she'd wish to choose for herself, rather than rely on Brad's selection. Amanda would *know* the type of ring she wanted. It would be something expensive and showy enough to catch the eye from the other side of the room.

But when Delcie reached the shop door she paused uncertainly, hesitating to go in because Brad appeared to be engrossed in what was obviously private business. He stood with his back partly turned to her, gazing into a small box held by the assistant, and from above their heads a lowered electric light brought a flash of brilliant sparkle from the box. Little imagination was needed for her to guess it contained a diamond ring.

So Amanda had been right. He *had* been ordering an engagement ring, perhaps to be made from stones he had personally selected. And then his remark to his mother swept into Delcie's mind. Was it only yesterday he had assured her that *everything would be all right*?

Her thoughts then went to Amanda who was with Richard Dillon, and suddenly the situation as she knew it made her feel ill. She moved away from the doorway before Brad could see her, then began an aimless wandering from shop to shop. She hardly saw the goods offered for sale, and eventually she found a seat where she sat and waited until it was time to collect the cufflinks. And as the minutes slipped past her mind worked to sort out the state of affairs between Amanda and Brad.

Ticking off the points one by one, Delcie recalled that Amanda, by her attentions to Richard Dillon, had sought to make Brad jealous. Apparently she had succeeded because it now seemed clear that Brad had at last decided he would marry her. But in the meantime Richard and Amanda had taken more than a fancy to each other, their attitudes of intimacy in the restaurant being mute evidence of this fact. But was there any real depth to it?

Delcie hated the thought of seeing Brad hurt by Amanda, and her own love for him caused her sympathy to gush towards him. Granted, Amanda had waited a long time for Brad to ask her to marry him, but he had had to be sure of his own feelings towards her, hadn't he? Excuses for him swirled about in her mind.

And then came another question. When did he intend to offer the ring to Amanda? *Of course*—it would be at the Christmas party. No doubt he intended to announce their engagement when all their friends were present. She sighed as she became overwhelmed by her own bitter disappointment.

But who knew what would happen? she asked herself. Did Amanda really love Richard, or was it only a brief infatuation? Had her interest been caught by his house and its antiques? Depressed, Delcie left the seat and walked back to the jeweller's shop. She collected and paid for the cufflinks which were waiting for her, then returned to where her car was parked and drove home.

As the day of the party drew near Delcie noticed that Joan Bellamy's mood became increasingly gloomy, and it wasn't difficult to guess that it had been caused by Amanda'a constant absence, although this was not verified until one afternoon when Joan came into the office.

'My dear,' she almost pleaded, 'I hate to disturb you when I can see you're so busy, but would you help me

with the Christmas tree. Sally and her mother are fully
occupied in the kitchen and—and——' She faltered and
fell silent.

'And Amanda isn't here,' Delcie finished for her. The
appeal in the older woman's voice told her she was being
looked upon as a last resort.

'Exactly. She appears to be avoiding us and I'd like to
know why.' The piercing stare she sent Delcie demanded
an answer.

'I know you think it's my fault,' Delcie said with all the
cool dignity she could muster.

Joan Bellamy sighed. 'I'm afraid I no longer know
what to think. Amanda has decorated our tree for years.
Why not this year?'

Delcie hesitated, then asked, 'Is it possible she could
have found an interest—elsewhere?'

Joan's voice became cold. 'Are you suggesting she's
looking at some man other than Brad? You'd have to be
joking, of course.' Then, brushing the question aside as
though it couldn't be more ridiculous, her tone changed
as she went on briskly, 'Well, do you intend to help me or
not?'

'Yes, I'd love to do the tree,' Delcie admitted frankly,
her eyes shining at the mere thought.

She left the typewriter without making any attempt to
hide her eagerness, then followed Joan to where a young
Douglas fir stood in a tub beside the lounge fireplace. Its
straight trunk gave promise of a tall tree in years to come,
but at present its dark green horizontal branches were
entirely suitable for bearing the decorations and two sets
of coloured lights that would be plugged into the twin
wall bracket.

Joan had already carried in the kitchen steps which
enabled Olga Brown to reach the higher cupboards, and
beside them sat the boxes of baubles waiting to be
attached to the branches.

For the next hour Delcie really enjoyed herself. She
climbed the steps and stretched her arms to entwine the

strings of lights through the foliage, and next came the addition of coloured glass bells, balls, reindeer and other small shining animals. There were long strands of fluffy silver tinsel which glittered like fairy froth when the lights were turned on, angels with gossamer wings, and a star for the top of the tree.

Joan attached a few coloured balls to the lower branches, but spent most of the time standing back to observe Delcie's activities. 'You do everything so efficiently,' she said with what was almost a hint of resentment in her voice.

Delcie attached the star to the top of the tree, then came down the ladder. 'Do you think it's all right?' she asked anxiously.

Joan stared at the tree in silence, then conceded reluctantly, 'Yes. I'm sure it looks—quite nice—but not as good——'

'But not as good as Amanda's efforts,' Delcie was goaded to reply. After all, what else could she expect?

'Well, my dear, Amanda is so very artistic.'

Delcie's spirits took a downward turn. She had tried to put thought into the decorating of the tree, but apparently Joan Bellamy was not impressed by the result. 'You don't like it?' she asked nervously, her eyes shadowed by disappointment.

But before Joan could reply Brad spoke from behind them. 'Ah, I see the tree is under control.' He stood staring at it.

'What do you think of it?' Joan asked, inviting his criticism.

He continued to examine it in silence, his eyes slightly narrowed.

His mother went on, 'You'll recall that Amanda always placed the angels on the outer branches where they looked so sweet.'

'But Delcie has grouped them up under the star,' he said thoughtfully. 'She's realised that unity is strength, and she's made a focal point of them. Somehow there's something quite significant in the way she's turned their heads to look up at the star. A great improvement, I think.'

Joan's jaw dropped slightly. 'Oh, I see what you mean.'

'And I like the way she's handled the balls and bells by placing the complementary colours within a cooee of each other, the reds near the greens, the yellows verging towards the purples, the blues and orange. It makes a change from the previous haphazard scattering of baubles. Yes, Delcie has to be congratulated on the effort.'

Delcie felt her cheeks become pink as Brad's words of praise made her heart glow, but at the same time she noticed that Joan's lips had thinned into a line of disapproval, so she made a hasty retreat to the office.

When the day of the party dawned, Delcie found herself beset by a variety of emotions, none of which did anything towards giving her peace of mind. From early morning depression held her in a firm grip because she felt sure that this evening would be the time when Amanda would be offered a ring. No doubt Brad would draw her out towards the rose-covered archway in the garden, and when they came in the announcement would be made.

She washed her hair, and as she set it in rollers she tortured herself by wondering if she'd be able to keep a bright face before the numerous guests. She knew she would have to kiss both Brad and Amanda while wishing them happiness, and she would have to smile while her heart shed tears. And if she escaped to her room, the guests would notice her absence. Eyebrows could be raised and questions asked.

During the day she caught only fleeting glimpses of Brad, although on one occasion as they passed in the hall he surprised her by pausing to say, 'Tonight you must wear that filmy lilac-pink affair you wore at Otaki.'

She gaped at him. 'You actually remember what I wore at Otaki?'

'Of course. Who could forget a sugar-plum fairy?'

Rebellion arose within her. 'You're laughing at me,' she accused, her lip quivering slightly. 'And you dare to tell me what to wear when you're about to—to——' The words faded unspoken.

His eyes narrowed as he stared at her. 'Yes? When I'm about to what?'

But she was unable to look at him. 'Nothing,' she mumbled as she swung round and hurried up the stairs, her soul filled with misery. What an ass she'd almost made of herself.

His voice floated up to her. 'If I didn't have so much on my plate I'd wring it out of you,' he shouted as she reached the top and ran towards her room.

Indignation was still bubbling as she put on the sleeveless fuschia with the knife-pleated skirt, and although she told herself she didn't care how she looked she found herself putting on more make-up than usual and taking extra care over her hair.

When she went downstairs the sight of Brad waiting to receive his guests almost took her breath away. He looked so handsome in his dark, well-cut suit that she found difficulty in dragging her eyes from his virile form, and in keeping her mind from his embodied masculinity which seemed to reach out and draw her towards him. But this almost overwhelming desire to move nearer to him was controlled by turning her attention to Joan, who looked regal in an expensive dress of midnight blue.

Olga Brown and Sally came into the room, both dressed in their best, and as the guests began to arrive Delcie found herself being introduced to the farm manager and three shepherds and their wives. It was then she realised that Brad looked upon his staff as his friends, rather more than mere labourers on the property, ranking them beside his more affluent neighbours and acquaintances.

Within a short time the rooms were full of guests, the buzz of conversation filling the air as old friends mingled and chatted. Small hot savouries were handed round and glasses were kept filled.

When the Dillons arrived, Delcie was introduced to Richard's father, a tall, broad-shouldered man who was an older and more rugged version of his son. And as Mary kissed her warmly she said, 'Derek has been through his old movie reels and he's found it—the one with your parents. We're so thankful it hadn't been discarded. I'll talk to you later. You must come out to see it.'

Delcie nodded wordlessly, then found herself engulfed in Richard's arms while he gave her what could only be termed a brotherly hug. As he released her she became aware of Brad watching them from across the room, but before she could begin to wonder about the dark scowl on his face her attention was drawn towards Amanda, who had just arrived.

Looking dazzling in brilliant red, the tall dark-eyed girl was now making a theatrical entrance by posing in the doorway while calling and waving to friends in the room. Brad went forward to greet her with a light kiss, and then Richard joined them to draw Amanda aside.

Watching them, Delcie tried to gauge Brad's reaction to this move but her study of his face was interrupted by a light touch on the arm. She turned to face an elderly man with a gleaming bald head and sharp blue eyes that twinkled beneath bushy brows.

'I know who you are,' he said. 'You're Denise all over again.'

'And you're Mr Pringle!' she exclaimed, recognising the solicitor who handled her affairs.

'You should've been to see me ages ago,' he chided. 'That day when I called, we didn't see much of each other. How's that battleaxe Lois? Still grinding her teeth, I suppose?'

Delcie laughed. 'I don't know. I haven't seen her for a

few weeks, nor am I her top favourite at present—not that I ever was.'

'What have you done to earn her displeasure?'

She hesitated, then admitted, 'Well, we should be away on holiday, instead of which I'm here.'

His eyes became piercing. 'How did that particular miracle come about?'

Again Delcie hesitated. 'It's a long story. There was an—an accident during which I caused Brad to hurt his hand. It put him out of action for typing. Aunt Lois has always drummed the word duty into me so I decided it was my duty to help him.'

'*You* decided—or *he* decided?' The blue eyes had become shrewd.

'Well, I suppose he decided, really.' She gave a brief explanation of what had happened.

Luke Pringle began to chuckle. 'Are you telling me he arrived at the house and stood up to Lois?'

She nodded. 'And I came home with him.'

'Well, I'll be damned! I must shake his hand! It calls for congratulations.' He paused as he looked at her searchingly. 'Is there something I've missed? Something else for which congratulations are due?'

She flushed as she shook her head. 'Not as far as I'm concerned, but perhaps later this evening—who knows?'

The elderly solicitor glanced across the room to where Brad was again talking to Amanda. Something about their attitude caused him to frown and utter darkly, 'Who knows? You're not telling me it's that witch?'

She bit her lip, appalled by the stage the discussion had reached, 'Mr Pringle, I really don't know.'

He went on throughtfully, 'Everyone knows it's been his mother's wish for a long time, and this is a large gathering of friends. A big party is always a good occasion for an announcement——'

'Really, *I don't know*.' Her voice shook slightly.

He sent her a sharp glance. 'But you *fear*?' His voice now held sympathy.

Despite herself she nodded miserably, and even as their eyes turned again towards the pair under discussion they saw Amanda take Brad's arm and draw him towards the front hall.

And then she became aware of Richard at her side begging her to come and dance on the verandah where coloured lights gave an aura of gaiety. The long summer evening was now fading into darkness, but even so it was still light enough to see Brad and Amanda walking across the lawn towards the rose gardens. The sight of them caused Delcie's heart to sink. Everything was happening as she had predicted in her own mind.

Richard followed her glance. 'Those two have something to talk about,' he remarked easily.

'They have?' Delcie looked up at him, awaiting more information. 'Something really important?'

'Sure. I'd say it's important,' he grinned.

She continued to stare at him, her eyes full of questions. 'Are you saying you know what they're talking about?'

'I reckon I can make a fairly close guess at it. Are you going to dance, or do you intend to stand there pretending to be a marble statue?'

She pulled herself together by dragging her mind away from the rose garden, and as they swayed to the rhythm of the tape-recorded music she made an effort to respond to Richard's cheerful but inconsequential small talk.

She must have been mistaken, she thought, recalling his attitude towards Amanda when in the restaurant. Apparently it meant little to him that she was now out there with Brad and that when they came in they'd be engaged. But to her surprise Richard stopped dancing to stare into the gathering gloom.

'I knew Brad wouldn't neglect his guests for long,' he said. 'They're coming back now.'

Delcie's eyes went to the two figures crossing the lawn. 'Well, *that* didn't take long,' she remarked, her voice betraying surprise. She watched as they approached the steps but could see no hint of suppressed excitement, although Amanda was smiling happily.

Richard's brows rose. 'Take long?' No. Why should it?'

Vaguely she wondered if their minds were on the same subject. 'I'd have thought a little more time could've been spent——' Her words died as Brad and Amanda stepped on to the verandah.

Amanda was still smiling as she stretched a hand towards Richard. 'Come and find a drink for me,' she said gaily. 'I'm sure Delcie can spare you.'

Delcie hardly heard the words or noticed Richard leave her side. Her eyes had become riveted upon Amanda's left hand—but there was no ring on it. Not the vestige of a sparkle. Did this mean they hadn't become engaged? It seemed as though there would be no dreaded announcement this evening, and suddenly the anticlimax of it all sent her spirits soaring to the heights. Her face glowed and her eyes shone, while the blessed relief from her previous tension gave her an inane desire to giggle.

'Your dancing partner appears to have deserted you,' said Brad. 'Shall we finish the music on this tape? It's a pity to waste a slow waltz,' he added, leading her on to the dancing area.

As they glided to the rhythm of the haunting melody she said, 'It's a lovely tune. What is it,?'

'Destiny Waltz. It's very old.'

'*Destiny?* Then it's wrongly named.'

He was surprised by the force behind her words. 'You think so? Why, for Pete's sake?'

'Because destiny is one's lot in life, and one's lot is seldom as soothing and beautiful as that music.'

He continued to look down at her. 'It's said that destiny leads the willing but drags the unwilling. Does this mean you're beginning to find your own lot a bit of a bore?'

'It could be better,' she retorted unguardedly.

'In what way?' he demanded, then before she could

answer he said, 'Yes, I know you lost your parents, but you've much to be thankful for. You're young and, I think, more beautiful than you realise, and you appear to have a good job——'

'You're right. I'm being a fool. But there are other things, you know—things that matter greatly.'

'Such as?' The brown eyes held questions.

She shook her head and remained silent. How could she tell him that the man she loved was not holding her closely while they waltzed to that soft dreamy music? His chin was not pressing against her forehead, offering that touch of sweet intimacy for which she craved. Nor, in future, would there be any more of those unexpected kisses because, despite the lack of a ring, there *had* to be something between Amanda and this man. But what?

Making an effort to hide her curiosity she smiled up at him and remarked casually, 'Amanda looked happy when she came up the steps with you.'

'Did she? I really didn't notice. Well, I suppose she's happy enough now.' His tone was non-committal.

Searchingly she looked up into his eyes. 'There must be a reason for it.'

He gave a chuckle that rumbled deeply in his throat. 'Oh, yes, there's a reason for it. You'll know all about it when the announcement's made.'

Her heart sank to zero. 'Oh. So there *is* to be an announcement tonight? I'll admit I was wondering about it.'

'No, not tonight. Amanda doesn't consider tonight a suitable occasion. She'd prefer the engagement to be announced at a party in her own home. Her parents will put on the show, you understand.'

'Yes, I suppose so.' Depression made her lose concentration on the rhythm. Her steps faltered, and as she regained the time of the music she lowered her head, resting it against his shoulder before he could read the misery in her eyes.

'It'll probably be a big New Year's Eve affair with half the world there,' he added.

'A show of shows, no doubt.' It was difficult to keep the bitterness from her voice. So this was what Brad and Amanda had been discussing beneath the archway of roses, she thought. At the same time she decided that, even if invited, she would not attend the function. An excuse would have to be found—a headache, or—or *something*. Then, common sense prevailing, she decided to cross that bridge when she came to it.

When the music ended Brad turned the tape in the recorder, then said with a slightly apologetic smile, 'I'm afraid I've been neglecting my guests. It's time I returned to them.'

'Of course.' She followed him inside where the loud hum of chatter now made conversation difficult, and looking round the lounge she saw Luke Pringle watching her intently.

He approached and drew her away to the quieter area of the living-room where he said, 'I saw you dancing with Brad. I wondered if he told you there's to be an announcement.'

She shook her head. 'No, not tonight. Perhaps at New Year.'

'I see.' He paused while his sharp blue eyes fixed her with a steady stare. 'Well now, there's one thing I want you to remember. When the day of your own wedding has been arranged you must come and see me in my office.'

She was puzzled. 'Oh? Why?'

'Because, my dear, when you leave your aunts' home adjustments will have to be made to your financial affairs.'

'You mean——'

'I mean it will be no longer necessary for you to carry that household on your back.'

She began to protest. 'But how will they manage?'

'Easily,' he snapped. 'That cry of poverty from Lois is

a lot of codswallop. I was fooled by it at first, but not any longer. They have more money than you realise. I know because I made it my business to find out. It's just that they prefer to use your money rather than their own.'

Delcie smiled whimsically. 'At least it's nice to know I've paid my own way.'

'You can put a ring round that particular statement,' he retorted grimly. 'However, when you marry, the spending of all your dividends will be in your own hands. What you do with the money will be up to you. Do you understand?'

'Yes. Thank you, Mr Pringle, but I don't think I'll be getting married for a very long time—that's if I ever do.' She sighed, feeling suddenly weary.

'Don't be too sure about that, my dear.' His eyes twinkled. 'So remember, if by some strange miracle you do happen to find Mr Right, we'll soon find the money for the type of wedding your parents would have wanted for you. One with all the trimmings.'

She nodded, unable to say more than a mumbled, 'Thank you, Mr Pringle. You've been very kind to me. I appreciate it.'

'I was very fond of your parents, my dear. They were a charming young couple.' He blinked rapidly, cleared his throat and moved away to speak to other friends.

Delcie thought of his words. *All the trimmings*. She knew that this meant a beautiful white bridal gown with a long trailing veil, a bouquet, perhaps of Christmas lilies, the church decorated with flowers and Brad waiting for her at the altar. Only it wouldn't be Brad, it would be somebody else.

The rest of the evening passed hazily as she chatted to people while fighting an overwhelming depression, and it was really Mary Dillon who brought her back to a more cheerful frame of mind.

Touching Delcie on the arm she said, 'Derek and I are leaving now, dear. He's had a long day with haymakers and is rather tired. However, they finished today and I was wondering about tomorrow. Would you like to come out and see that film?'

Delcie looked at her gratefully as the suggestion lifted her out of the gloom. It gave her something different to think about and an inner excitement grew as her mind contemplated the film with her parents on it. She would actually see what they looked like—how they walked, how they smiled. *They'd be alive.* She swallowed and said huskily, 'Yes, please. It would be so—so wonderful.'

Mary looked at her with a depth of understanding. 'It'll be an emotional experience for you, my dear. I'm wondering if you'd like to bring Joan with you, or if you'd rather come alone.'

'I—I'd rather come alone, if you don't mind.'

'Very well. You're sure you can find your way?'

'I think so. You said your place is the next on the left past Richard's entrance. I'll find it.'

'Then I'll expect you about mid-afternoon. Derek has a special dark room for showing films in the daytime. Now I must find him and say goodnight to Joan and Brad. It's been a lovely party.'

Has it? Delcie wondered vaguely as she watched Mary draw her husband from a group of men who argued volubly about new methods in the farming world.

The Dillons' departure acted as a signal for others to leave, and when the last guest had gone Delcie helped Olga and Sally to put the rooms in order. Chairs were pushed back to their normal positions, glasses were carried out to the kitchen, and not until the last of the coffee cups and savoury plates had been put through the dishwasher did she contemplate going upstairs to bed.

She was crossing the hall when Brad waylaid her. Despite the lateness of the hour he showed no sign of fatigue, and her knees felt weak as he drew her out on to the verandah. Her heart flipped as he turned her towards him, his hands cupping her face while his head bent to brush her lips with what could only be termed a chaste brotherly kiss.

'Thank you, Delcie,' he murmured huskily.

The reason for his gratitude escaped her. She looked at him wonderingly then asked, 'Thank you—for what?'

'For helping to make the party a success. Mother always becomes engrossed with her old cronies, and I watched while you concentrated on the wives of those young shepherds. Your efforts made them feel welcome, I think.'

'I could see they felt shy about being invited into the boss's home for the first time.'

'So you put them at ease and I'm grateful. Tomorrow you're to have a rest. You're to sleep in and not to go near the office. That is an order and I intend to see it's obeyed.'

She laughed. 'Thank you, boss, but tomorrow is already planned. I intend to type in the morning and visit the Dillons in the afternoon. I'm to see the film that shows my parents.' A hint of excitement had crept into her voice.

'Mother and Amanda are going with you?'

'No. I'm going alone.'

'Are you saying Mary didn't invite them? If I remember correctly. Amanda made no secret of being keen to see those home movies.'

Delcie gave a faint smile. 'Mary is very understanding. She knows I'll probably become upset and that I'll have no wish for an audience for my tears. Besides, neither your mother nor Amanda are even remotely interested in my parents.'

'Would it surprise you to learn that I could be interested in seeing your parents.'

'It would indeed. I can understand you being interested in Amanda's parents, but not mine.'

'Nevertheless I intend to come with you.'

She faced him squarely. 'Why?'

'Because I want to make sure you drive home safely. It'll be a traumatic experience and your mind could wander.'

'You're hinting that history could repeat itself? Don't worry, I won't roll the car.' She paused, then added firmly, 'Thank you for worrying about me, but really, I'd rather go alone.'

'You're sure about that?'

She nodded. 'I couldn't feel more definitely sure about it.'

'Very well. I'll respect your wishes, You'll find your way?'

'Yes. The turn-off at Carterton is well signposted.'

'Then go to bed and get some sleep.'

She looked up at him, half expecting to be kissed again, but he made no move to hold her against him. Instead he stood with his arms folded across his chest while he frowned and appeared to contemplate the gloomy shadows of the garden.

She left him standing on the verandah, and as she climbed the stairs a sigh escaped her. He's thinking of Amanda, she decided. Obviously her own power to arouse his desire to be close to her had vanished.

CHAPTER TEN

WHEN Delcie woke the next morning, instinct seemed to whisper that it would be a day to remember. She stretched in the bed, then lay still to stare at the ceiling while her mind wandered among the people she'd met at the party.

The farming staff had taken a special interest in her, and it had been easy to guess at the questions sizzling in their minds. Was it possible she could supplant Amanda? Was she to be the next mistress at Bellairs?

She had longed to herd them into a corner and shout the answers that would put their minds at rest. No, she could not supplant Amanda, and no, she was not to be the next mistress of Bellairs, but for confirmation of these facts they would have to wait until New Year when the announcement would be made.

She sighed deeply, then pushed the thought of Amanda from her mind. Amanda was not going to spoil this day for her.

When she went downstairs, Olga Brown told her that Mrs Bellamy would remain in bed for the morning, but that Brad was already in his office. 'As for you, you don't look at all tired,' the housekeeper added.

Nor did she feel weary. Anticipation seemed to buoy her spirits, lifting them from the sea of deep depression that was perilously near. However, she did not linger over breakfast, and when she went into the office she found Brad scribbling rapidly, his head bent over a pad.

He looked up briefly. 'Good morning, blue eyes. You're bright and early for one who's had a heavy night.'

She ignored his teasing to add a little of her own. 'You've been working since daybreak, I suppose?'

'Not exactly, but long enough to have taken stock of

what more there is to do. Your speedy typing will enable
the book to be finished well ahead of schedule. Would
you believe there are only three more chapters to be
done?'

Her heart sank. Three more chapters and she would
return to Wellington and the bosom of Aunt Lois where
all this would become like a dream. Three more chapters
and there'd be no reason for her to remain at Bellairs. But
after all, how could she possibly stay and watch loving
glances pass between Brad and Amanda? After New
Year the affection between them must surely become
evident.

He passed a number of handwritten sheets of paper to
her. 'OK, if you're determined to work this morning you
might as well get on with these.'

She took the pages gratefully, thankful to be able to
add them to the pile already drafted and waiting to be
typed. It was sufficient to keep her mind well occupied,
but before settling down to work she was unable to resist
a remark.

'Amanda looked really beautiful last night.'

'Amanda always looks beautiful,' he replied with a
smile.

'That red dress seemed to make her glow. She has a
real flair for clothes.'

There was no reply.

Work continued until after midday when Sally tapped
discreetly on the office door. 'Your mother is now
downstairs,' she informed Brad. 'She's in the dining-
room waiting to serve lunch.'

He stood up and stretched his long limbs. 'Thank you,
Sally. Tell her we're coming at once. I'm feeling peckish.'

Joan sent them a wan smile as they entered the room.
'I've slept for most of the morning but I'm still feeling
weary,' she admitted as she served crisp lettuce salad on
to her plate. Then, glancing at Brad, 'You'll be busy in
that office for the whole afternoon, I suppose.'

'That's right. Delcie types so rapidly it's difficult to keep ahead of her.'

Joan yawned delicately. 'I'd have enjoyed being taken for a drive. I need a breath of air.'

'Why not take yourself for a drive?' he queried.

'Because I'd like to be driven. I want to just sit and relax while I look at the countryside. It would be so soothing.' She turned to Delcie, her reluctance evident as she said, 'I suppose you'll be stuck in that office all the afternoon?'

'No. As it happens I'm going out.'

'Oh? Where to, may I ask?' Joan eyed her curiously.

'Is Delcie to be allowed no privacy at all?' Brad drawled.

Delcie felt she had no option but to explain her plans, so she said quietly, 'This afternoon I'm visiting Mrs Dillon.'

'Indeed? When was this arranged?' Joan's tone had become sharp.

'Last night. She said to come this afternoon.'

Joan stared at her disbelievingly. 'Are you saying that Mary Dillon asked *you* to visit her, but she didn't invite *me*?'

'It's to see the reel showing my parents,' Delcie explained.

Joan brightened visibly. 'Oh. Well I'll come with you. And I recall that Amanda was also keen to see it. I'll phone her——'

Delcie was appalled by the suggestion. Her irritation deepened sufficiently to make her assert herself and say firmly, 'If you don't mind, Mrs Bellamy, I'd rather go alone.'

'Are you hinting that you don't want us to come with you?' Joan snapped indignantly.

Delcie forced herself to smile. 'Yes, I am. I want to go alone—if you'll excuse me,' she finished politely.

Joan's mouth became set in a determined line. 'Nevertheless, I intend to go with you.'

Brad interrupted sharply. 'Mother, can't you see that if Mary had wanted you and Amanda to accompany Delcie she would've invited you both. She had plenty of opportunity last night.'

Joan shrugged. 'It probably slipped her memory.'

'She's had all the morning to phone you,' he pointed out.

She smiled at him. 'I *know* Mary, she'll just expect us to arrive with Delcie——' Her words were cut short by the loud ringing of the phone. 'Ah, that'll be her now.' Full of confidence she left the table.

Brad turned to Delcie and spoke earnestly. 'If you're really determined to go alone you'd be well advised to get into your car and slip away without a word.' He then fell silent as Joan's voice, raised in surprise, echoed clearly from the phone in the hall.

'No, he hasn't said a word. Yes, yes, of course I'll be here. Come as soon as you can and tell me all about it. *What?* Did you say New Year's Eve?'

When Joan returned to the room her manner had completely changed. Her face was alight with smiles as she went to Brad and placed a fond kiss on his brow while he sat at the table. 'My darling boy, why didn't you tell me?'

'Tell you what, Mother?' The brown eyes held a mischievous glint as they regarded her.

'About the engagement, of course, and the party at New Year.' She drew a deep breath of complete satisfaction. 'Really, I feel so excited about it all.'

Brad became slightly impatient. 'Mother, would you please calm down and tell me what was said on the phone. You were speaking to Amanda, I presume?'

'No, it was her mother.' She turned to Delcie. 'You met Elizabeth Stafford last night. She was the tall one in green.'

Delcie was surprised. 'Do you mean the one who chatted almost non-stop? I thought she seemed rather worked up about something.'

'I'm afraid she's inclined to be excitable. On the phone she was in such a state I could hardly understand what she was saying except that she had news for me and that the announcement would be made at the New Year's Eve party. Of course I knew what she meant by *news*.' Joan swept a fond glance over her son, then added, 'She's coming this afternoon to talk about it.'

'Amanda's coming with her?' Brad asked with an amused smile.

'No. Elizabeth said that Amanda was out visiting and that she'd be coming alone.' Joan's eyes turned again to Delcie. 'So you see I'll not be able to go with you after all.'

Delcie hoped that the relief in her mind didn't show too clearly on her face. At the same time she felt slightly sick with a depressing misery that made her anxious to be out of the house before Amanda's mother arrived. She had no wish to observe the excited satisfaction of the two mothers as they talked over a guest list and made arrangements for the engagement party.

Brad's voice hit her ears. 'What's the matter? You've gone very pale. Are you all right?'

Joan glanced at her briefly. 'She's tired after last night,' was all she said.

Delcie agreed hastily. 'Perhaps, a little. Otherwise I'm all right, thank you.' She became aware that Brad's eyes had narrowed slightly and that they held curiosity as they regarded her, so as soon as it was reasonably possible to do so, she left the table and hurried upstairs.

A cold wet cloth pressed to her eyes soaked up the burning tears and helped her to muster control. And as she changed into a dress that was more suitable for visiting she was thankful to have a reason for getting out of the house for a few hours.

A short time later it was a relief to be speeding along the country road towards the Tararua ranges, and as she approached the old home her parents had owned she stopped at the spot from which it could be seen.

Staring towards the view of red roofs and white

timbers she was tempted to drive in and take a quick peep, then decided against it, beause she might meet Richard and be delayed. Instead, she would call in to look at it on the way home. No doubt it would be the last time she would ever see it because her task at Bellairs was almost finished and the sooner she left that place the better it would be for her own peace of mind.

The next entrance on the left was soon reached, and as she stopped the car near the front door of the single-story wide-fronted house Mary Dillon came out to greet her warmly.

'I see you've managed to come alone,' she said with a smile. 'I felt sure Joan would insist upon coming with you.'

'She has a visitor this afternoon,' Delcie said without further explanation, her mind shying away from the discussion she knew would be taking place at Bellairs.

'Oh. Well, Derek's got the projector set up in his dark room, but we'll have a cup of tea first. We won't linger over it because I know what you're longing to see, but Derek always has his tea at this hour.'

A short time later Delcie was led along a passage to a room occupied by Derek's photographic equipment. A projector was set in position to throw pictures on a screen hung on the far wall, and a row of chairs enabled viewers to sit and watch the results of his work with the camera.

His jovial voice came to her through the gloom. 'I'm afraid you'll have to sit through the first part of the reel which features Richard when he was a boy. Your parents are near the end of it.'

'Yes, I understand.' The thought that she was soon to see them made her breath quicken with a surge of excitement.

'I'm afraid I didn't have colour film in those days,' Derek added regretfully. 'These are only black and white.'

She nodded, understanding, and as the screen flashed to life she watched a young Richard riding his pony on the farm, jumping over low hurdles, even grooming it at the stables. She saw him entertaining boys at his birthday party and playing cricket in the field. There were antics with his fox terrier to be viewed. In fact the shots featuring Richard seemed endless, almost causing Delcie to fidget with impatience. However, she managed to control herself.

At last Derek said, 'Ah, here we are——'

The scene had changed abruptly from farmland to a small clearing in the bush. There was a grassy area surrounded by tall dark trees, and beside it bubbled a narrow stony stream. Richard and a younger Mary sat on a rug near an open picnic hamper, while a man, a woman and a small child sat with their backs towards the camera.

Frustrated, Delcie waited for them to turn so that she could see their faces; it was the child who scrambled to her feet first and toddled towards the stream. '*That's me!*' she gasped, staring at the small round face and bobbing curls.

'And a cuddly little bundle you were,' Derek commented gruffly.

She hardly heard his words, her eyes widened as she sat bolt upright to watch the woman rise to her feet and hurry after the child. No mirror was necessary to show that the likeness to herself was incredible, nor was Mary's whispered 'There's Denise,' really needed.

Fascinated, Delcie watched as her mother swept her small self up into her arms, then found herself smiling at her own naughty kicking and obvious yelling. And then the man sitting on the rug rose to his feet to cross the grass and take the protesting child from Denise's arms.

Delcie knew she was looking at her father—the man referred to by Aunt Lois as 'that fellow'. Regarding him critically, she decided that his pleasant face was really quite handsome, and she could understand her mother falling in love with him.

Yet although she knew that these two people were her

parents, the tears she had expected to shed did not come
to her eyes. Instead she found herself beset by other
emotions, the foremost being an intense interest in their
appearance, coupled with an excitement and deep
gratitude at being able to see them alive and moving on
the screen.

At the same time she felt strangely detached, finding it
almost impossible to believe they actually *were* her
parents, but perhaps this was because she had never
really known them. She had been too young to remember
their faces, so they had left no definite pictures in her
mind.

She watched as they returned to sit on the rug, and as
Mary became busy with a Thermos flask the film ended.

'That's where Mary called me for tea,' Derek said
regretfully.

He ran the latter part of the film several times for her,
but at last she knew she must leave. She wanted to think
about the two people she had watched on the screen, and
the desire for another look at the home in which they had
lived was now even stronger than when she had first
arrived. With this in mind she said, 'Do you think
Richard is at home? I'd love to look at the old house just
once more.'

Derek said, 'He's sure to be away out on the farm.'

But Mary added, 'The woman who keeps house for
him is away for a few days, but if Richard isn't there you
have our permission to walk in and look through the
rooms. I know he'd be glad for you to do so. I only wish
that you and he——' She sighed then fell silent.

Delcie knew what she meant but made no reply apart
from thanking them for enabling her to see her parents.
Moments later she was driving along the road towards
Richard's place where she stopped the car at the
entrance. She got out and stared at the name Linden,
then walked slowly along the drive.

Wandering round the house she examined flowers and
shrubs, but the garden was deserted. However, the back

door was open and she stepped into the kitchen where a few unwashed dishes were stacked on the bench.

From the kitchen she went through to the lounge where she sat for several moments, the screen images of her parents vividly before her mind. Everything seemed so silent and she began to feel like a trespasser, but before she left she had to take a quick peep in the upper rooms. After all, Derek and Mary had given their permission.

Still obsessed by the feeling that she shouldn't be there, she crept quietly up the stairs. The main bedroom she felt sure her parents would have used was straight ahead of her, but when she reached the door she was brought to an abrupt halt by a sight that shocked her. Hardly able to believe her eyes, she brought her hand quickly up to her mouth to stifle a gasp that rose to her lips.

The room was not empty. It was occupied by Richard and Amanda who were both asleep in the large double bed. Richard's arms encircled Amanda's slim form and her black tresses were spread across the pillow.

One horrified glance told Delcie all she needed to know. She turned and fled down the stairs, through the front door and along the drive to where she'd left her car at the entrance. She revved the motor and sped along the road.

Tears blurred her vision as she thought of the scene she had just witnessed. Richard and Amanda had obviously been making love, but in a short time Amanda was due to announce her engagement to Brad. How could she be so two-faced? How could she be so unfaithful to the man she professed to love?

The whole situation was beyond Delcie's comprehension, and as copious tears continued to fall she had to blink rapidly to see where she was going. She also realised she was driving too fast; unless she slackened speed she would suffer the same fate as her parents. As she approached the last bend of the hill they had gone over, the white protective railing caught her eyes. She stopped the car beside it because she wanted to think.

Something had to be done to save Brad from marrying Amanda, she realised, but what could she herself do about it? Nothing. Nothing at all. The thought of telling him about the scene in the bedroom made her cringe, and she knew she couldn't do it. Nor would he be likely to believe her.

She got out of the car and went to stand by the rail. The hill dropped sharply from it, and, looking down, she noticed a hump of limestone rock jutting from a small flat area. It was only a short distance below the road and seemed to offer a place of solitude where she could ponder the situation, or at least have a good cry before driving any further.

She reached it by climbing over the rail and slithering down the slope. Then, sitting with her back to the rock, her uncontrolled sobs broke forth until they shook her body. Most of the tears were for Brad because, loving him, she couldn't bear the thought of seeing him hurt. But when her eyes stared towards the bottom of the hill, the sobs turned to an agony of grief for her parents.

At last the spasm of weeping passed, and as she sat in exhausted silence she imagined she heard Brad's voice echo on the air. She blinked, then shook her head slowly, sure that her mind must be wandering. But no, it came again, and moments later he was beside her, his brown eyes full of concern.

'You've been having a darned good cry,' he observed. 'That's good. It gets it out of your system.'

She nodded, knowing that he presumed she had wept only for her parents. Then, surprised by his unexpected arrival, she asked, 'Why are you here?'

'I thought I'd come and meet you. I didn't know how you'd react to the sight of your parents on the screen and, to be honest, I felt worried about you.'

Astonished, she gaped at him. 'You felt worried about me?'

'Of course. Why not? Is it so unusual that I'd want to make sure you arrived home safely?'

'Thank you. I'm grateful that you should consider me when——' Further words failed her.

'Yes? When what?' His eyes questioned keenly.

'Well—when your thoughts are with Amanda, of course.'

He laughed. 'My thoughts have certainly been with Amanda this afternoon. What a scene,' he added inexplicably.

She was puzzled. 'Scene? I don't understand.'

'Can you imagine two mothers whose cherished plan has been spiked? I can tell you there's been much loud wailing, beating of breasts, gnashing of teeth——'

She was bewildered. 'Surely you're joking? There couldn't be all that fuss over a few party arrangements.'

'Perhaps I exaggerate slightly,' he conceded. 'However, there will be no engagement party. Amanda wants to get married at once. That, among other things, is what Elizabeth Stafford came to tell Mother. She was so anxious for Mother to understand.'

Delcie's heart sank. 'Oh. Well, she wouldn't find that too difficult.'

'Believe me, the news gave Mother a nasty shock.'

'Why should it? She's been longing for you to marry Amanda, so why all the loud wailing, etcetera?'

He turned to stare at her. 'My dear blue eyes, something tells me you're not with it. You don't seem to be aware of the situation. I'm not the bridegroom. Amanda is to marry Richard.'

'*Richard!*' The name echoed from her lips as she stared at him, wondering if she'd heard correctly.

'Haven't you noticed how things are between them?'

She recalled the day she had seen them together in the restaurant and, more recently, in the bed. 'Well, yes, I did wonder about it.' But apparently she hadn't given it enough thought.

'Last night I had definite confirmation of it from Amanda. She admitted that in her efforts to get him interested in you, she'd fallen in love with him herself. I don't know when I've felt so relieved about anything.' He gave a sudden carefree laugh.

'But—but you bought a ring for her.'

His brows rose. 'How do you know I bought a ring?'

'Because I saw you in the jeweller's shop. You were at a counter near the door and I saw you holding a small box. The flash of brilliance coming from it could've meant only one thing—an engagement ring. I expected you to give it to Amanda last night.'

'You're right about the fact that I bought a ring, but please believe me when I say it was never intended for Amanda.'

'Oh, I'm sorry. I didn't mean to pry.'

His hand went into his jacket pocket to draw forth a small red velvety box. 'Does this look like it?'

She felt embarrassed. 'Possibly. I—I really don't know.'

He flicked it open to reveal a sparkling cluster of high quality diamonds. 'I chose the stones myself,' he admitted. 'Do you like it? Would it be your choice?'

'Oh, yes—it's really beautiful,' she gasped. 'But if you didn't buy it for Amanda——'

'I must have bought it for you. That's if you'll accept it, of course.' He regarded her seriously. 'Will you marry me, Delcie? I love you very much.'

She nodded as he slipped it on her finger. 'Yes—oh, yes——' Then, unable to find more words, she stared in silence at the ring, hardly able to believe her eyes.

'Tell me you love me, my darling.'

'I love you, Brad. I love you deeply. I was so sure you must have guessed—that it had been written all over my face.'

'The only face I've seen is one that I've longed to kiss. You're so lovely, my darling.'

His arms were about her, pressing her back against the flat grassy area beside the limestone which sheltered them from the prying eyes of anyone passing on the road above. And as they lay with their bodies moulded closely against each other, she clung to him in a frenzy of sweet surrender.

His lips on hers became possessive, while his hands fondling her breasts to find raised nipples awakened every nerve and sent spasms of pleasure shooting through every fibre of her being. And as she responded to the call of his passion she was filled with a depth of longing to consummate their love there and then.

Almost as though her desire had pleaded aloud he said huskily, 'Not here, my beloved. This is neither the time nor the place. When I possess my dearest one I want her to be naked in the bed where I can kiss her all over.' He put her from him with reluctant but firm determination, then sat up abruptly. 'And that brings me to the burning question. How soon can we be married?'

'As soon as it can be arranged,' she replied, her mind coming down to earth through a haze of happiness.

'Aunt Lois presiding, I suppose?'

'Not necessarily. I can make all my own arrangements. Mr Pringle said that as soon as I've decided to marry I'm to go to him. She gasped. 'My goodness! That was only last night.'

'Things do pop out of the blue,' he reminded her soberly. 'Like meeting people on stairways——'

She lifted his right hand to her lips. 'And like having people bang on one's door next morning.'

'That was because I couldn't bear to lose sight of you so quickly.'

She was amazed. 'I thought I'd have been the last person you'd want to see again.'

He shook his head. 'After you'd gone I slept for a few hours, but at about three in the morning I woke with pain in my hand. I lay in the darkness with your face hovering about in my mind. I simply couldn't get rid of it, and I couldn't get to sleep again. You positively plagued me.'

'A real pest. You must have been infuriated with me!'

'On the contrary, all my previous fury with you had evaporated and I knew I had to see you again. I told myself I was an utter fool and being completely ridiculous, and that I'd feel differently in the morning, so I got out of bed and dosed myself with a couple of painkillers.'

'And in the morning?'

'Things were no better. In fact they were worse. Your face was still there, taunting me with lips that I'd already kissed. I became obsessed with the desire to kiss them again—and again.' He paused to draw her down to the turf, his arms crushing her to him as his mouth again found hers in urgent demand.

At last she smiled up at him. 'Tell me more. I'm starving for every little detail.'

'The idea came to me while I was shaving. I recalled that you'd told me you taught typing, and a typist was exactly what I'd be needing in a very short time. And then your scribbled address caught my eye, so I decided to bully you into coming home with me.'

She laughed. 'And a most successful bully were, especially having to cope with Aunt Lois. People don't normally stand up to her. They usually do exactly as she demands, or quail and run.'

'It was easy to see that you had never learnt to stand up to her. You needed a strong arm—one that would snatch you away.'

'Thank you for providing it,' she whispered against his lips. 'Strangely, I feel differently about her now. She seems less formidable from a distance. It's when she's close enough to glare at me that I begin to shiver.'

'That's all over now, my dearest.'

'Yes, but I'm afraid she won't be pleased when she hears about us——' The words died on her lips as another thought leapt into her mind, causing her to sit up and stare at him. 'Nor will your mother be amused by this situation! She'll never accept me in place of Amanda.'

'You have little to fear from Mother,' he replied with a confident smile.

'Oh?' Her eyes were full of doubt.

'As I said, there was quite a scene at home. As soon as Elizabeth Stafford had departed Mother began to rant and rave against the world in general. In fact she went so berserk that Olga Brown came into the living-room to try and calm her.'

'She succeeded?'

'She did indeed. She sailed into Mother without any preamble. She told her she was being a stupid woman who obviously had no love for her son, otherwise she wouldn't try to force him into marrriage for the sake of a lump of land. She also told Mother that if she was as fond of Amanda as she professed to be, she'd be happy the girl had found her true love before making the mistake of marrying me. Yes, Olga certainly had her say.'

Delcie smiled at the thought of Olga standing up to Joan Bellamy. 'What happened then?' she asked.

He laughed. 'It was my turn. Olga turned upon me. She declared that if I had eyes in my head I'd see that you were worth ten Amandas, and if I had any sense I'd marry you as soon as possible.'

Delcie gave a small giggle. 'What on earth did you say?'

'I told Olga that I intended to do just that. In fact I'd be leaving in a few minutes to go and find you, and to ask you to marry me. Olga then declared she was positive you loved me and that your answer would be yes.'

She drew a deep, contented sigh as his words rang like music in her ears. Nevertheless there was a question that still nagged. 'What did your mother say?'

'Nothing. She just sat with her mouth open. Gawping is the only word for it. And then Olga pointed out that perhaps I'd be wise to find a flat in Masterton for Mother. The suggestion was enough to bring Mother to life. She declared that I was to do no such thing, and that she was ready to welcome you with open arms.'

'She did? I can hardly believe it!'

'She went on to say that fate seemed to have sent you into her son's life, and it wasn't for her to interfere with destiny. Needless to say Olga and I were delighted. Olga said she would put the champagne on ice, and although it wasn't yet Christmas Day we'd cut the Christmas cake to celebrate. So would I please hurry and bring you home. You know, that woman is pure gold.'

She sat leaning against him, still in a happy daze. 'I'm finding difficulty in believing that any of this is true.' Then, shyly, 'When did you first begin to love me?'

'Right from the start, I think. As I began to know you my fears of that first night were confirmed. I was in love with you.'

'Yet you were determined that I should meet Richard. You pushed me at him. It was quite frustrating.'

'Can't you see? I was giving you the chance of falling for a man who could give you your old home. Any commitment between us had to come after you'd met Richard. I was terrified that you might really fall in love with him, or that the associations of your parents and the old home would prove strong enough to influence your affections towards him.'

'I understand. But you had nothing to fear. You're the only man I've ever wanted,' she admitted softly.

Her words were enough to send his arms about her again, and as his lips followed the line of her jaw, then descended to the cleavage at the low V of her dress, he muttered, 'Darling, if we don't go home I'll not be responsible for what could happen.'

She nodded. 'You're right, we must go before——' Confusion silenced her as she took his hand while scrambling up the steep slippery hillside to the road.

As Delcie drove home ahead of him it was only the sparkling cluster on her finger that assured her the last hour had not been a dream. She felt light-headed, and the excitement that engulfed her affected her driving. On one stretch she skidded slightly in loose metal and was rebuked by a volley of warning blasts from Brad's horn. It was enough to make her slacken speed, and at last she turned into the driveway of Bellairs, closely followed by Brad.

Here a surprise awaited them: they found themselves unable to reach the garage on account of numerous cars parked in the drive. And as they left their own cars to go towards the house the sound of gay chatter and laughter reached their ears.

Brad paused on the front steps to examine some of the vehicles. 'This looks like a staff gathering,' he said. 'And look, that's Luke Pringle's Mercedes. I believe Mother's been busy.' He put his arm about Delcie and drew her into the house.

They were greeted by loud cheers and applause while Joan came to kiss them both. Her smile was sincere as she said, 'I'm so happy for you. When Olga told me how many bottles of bubbly were over from last night I rang the staff and invited them to come and drink the health of the next bride at Bellairs.'

Brad's manager stepped forward to congratulate him. Glasses were raised and toasts were drunk.

Joan said, 'Olga pleaded against cutting the cake before you arrived. She declared you should do it together to make it the happiest Christmas ever. So if you'll just take this knife——'

As the pieces were being handed round, Luke Pringle came to Delcie's side. 'It looks as if you'll be coming to see me sooner than expected,' he grinned.

She nodded meekly, unable to speak as she looked at the smiling faces she'd met last night. And then Joan joined them.

The older woman said, 'My dear, Luke and I have been talking. He thinks it would be an excellent idea if Olga and I arranged the wedding for you. It would be in a church, of course, with a garden reception here at Bellairs, and quite soon if possible while the roses are still blooming. Would you like that?'

She could only nod. Everything was happening so quickly she felt she was being swept off her feet. Her dreams were crowding in upon her—it was like being offered the moon on a dish. Once again, only her engagement ring assured her that everything was real.

Later, when the farming staff and few close friends had departed, Joan said, 'I've been giving serious consideration to taking a flat in Masterton. Amanda once said she thought——'

Delcie cut in with a quick protest. 'I think that would be sad. Surely your place will always be here at Bellairs?'

Joan smiled. 'Newlyweds need the house to themselves. Besides, there's no reason for me to remain here.'

'There's one very good reason,' Delcie told her quietly. 'It's the fact that we want you to be with us. Please don't leave this place, I'll be most unhappy if you do.'

Joan's face reflected her amazement. 'My dear, are you really saying that you'd prefer me to stay?'

'Of course. I know so little about running a house. I'd be grateful if you'd teach me. Please, we'll *need* you.'

Brad sent his mother a look of quiet triumph. 'Didn't I tell you that everything would turn out all right? And Delcie's right when she says we really want you to be with us. Now, if you'll excuse us, we'd like to examine the roses by moonlight.'

'Of course. Off you go. Olga and I have so much to plan.'

Brad led Delcie down the front steps and across the lawn towards the heady perfume of the rose-covered archway where he took her in his arms. Overhead a full moon hung like a pale round face, casting shadows that enfolded them in a world of their own.

His lips found hers in a long kiss before he murmured, 'Thank you, my darling, thank you for everything.'

She gazed up at him, surprised by the gratitude in his voice. 'You're thanking me—for what?'

'For being like you are—capable, intelligent, and understanding enough to make my mother feel welcome to live with us. I love you for these things.'

'She's used to space,' Delcie pointed out. 'She'd go mad

in the confined area of a flat.'

'Amanda would have had her in one right smartly, and she knows it. Didn't she almost admit it?'

'Perhaps.'

He studied her through the gloom. 'Have you a special reason for wanting her to be with us?'

Her nod was almost imperceptible.

'Come on, let's share it,' he urged.

'I've always considered grandmothers to be handy people to have about the house,' she whispered shyly against his neck.

His kisses made further words impossible, and even the pale-faced moon seemed to smile.

Happy Mother's Day.

This Mother's Day, instead of the usual breakfast in bed, why not ask your family to treat you to the Mills & Boon Mother's Day pack. Four captivating romances to enthral you.

THE EMERALD SEA by Emily Spenser

A marine biologist finds herself out of her depth on an Italian film set — and with the director.

THE MARRIAGE BED by Catherine George

A holiday in the Algarve becomes a nightmare when the heroine is kidnapped in revenge for an injustice she knows nothing about.

AN IDEAL MATCH by Sandra Field

Despite two broken engagements, a young woman still believes in marriage — she comes to love a widower left with three children but finds he had lost his faith in love.

ROUGH DIAMOND by Kate Walker

Can a successful businesswoman and a garage mechanic really bridge the gap between two such different backgrounds?

FOUR UNIQUE LOVE STORIES IN A SPECIAL MOTHER'S DAY PACK AVAILABLE FROM FEBRUARY 1987.

PRICE £4.80.

Bewitched in her dreams she awoke to discover the face of reality

The same dark hair, the same mocking eyes. The Regency rake in the portrait, the seducer of Jenna's dreams had a living double.

But James Allingham was no dream, he was a direct descendant of the black sheep of the Deveril family.

They would fight for the possession of the ancestral home. They would fight against desire to be together.

Unravel the mysteries in
STRONGER THAN YEARNING,
a new longer romance from
Penny Jordan.

ROMANCE

Variety is the spice of romance

Each month, Mills & Boon publish new romances. New stories about people falling in love. A world of variety in romance — from the best writers in the romantic world. Choose from these titles in February.

ROSE-COLOURED LOVE Amanda Carpenter
GATHERING OF EAGLES Angela Carson
STREET SONG Ann Charlton
RECIPE FOR LOVE Kay Clifford
THE UNPREDICTABLE MAN Emma Darcy
THE MARRIED LOVERS Flora Kidd
A ROGUE AND A PIRATE Carole Mortimer
THE LOVE ARTIST Valerie Parv
SUNSET AT IZILWANE Yvonne Whittal
BRIDE OF DIAZ Patricia Wilson
***STAIRWAY TO DESTINY** Miriam MacGregor
***SLEEPING TIGER** Joanna Mansell

On sale where you buy paperbacks. If you require further information or have any difficulty obtaining them, write to: Mills & Boon Reader Service, PO Box 236, Thornton Road, Croydon, Surrey CR9 3RU, England.

*These two titles are available *only* from Mills & Boon Reader Service.

Mills & Boon
the rose of romance

ROMANCE

Next month's romances from Mills & Boon

Each month, you can choose from a world of variety in romance with Mills & Boon. These are the new titles to look out for next month.

THE HEART OF THE MATTER Lindsay Armstrong
KING OF THE HILL Emma Goldrick
A MAN OF CONTRASTS Claudia Jameson
TOO SHORT A BLESSING Penny Jordan
HIDE AND SEEK Charlotte Lamb
TOO BAD TO BE TRUE Roberta Leigh
DON'T ASK FOR TOMORROW S. McCarthy
STORMY SPRINGTIME Betty Neels
SHADOWS IN THE LIMELIGHT Sandra K. Rhoades
RELATIVE STRANGERS Jessica Steele
*UNTAMED SANCTUARY Annabel Murray
*LOVE UPON THE WIND Sally Stewart

Buy them from your usual paperback stockist, or write to: Mills & Boon Reader Service, P.O. Box 236, Thornton Rd, Croydon, Surrey CR9 3RU, England. Readers in Southern Africa — write to: Independent Book Services Pty, Postbag X3010, Randburg, 2125, S. Africa.

*These two titles are available *only* from Mills & Boon Reader Service.

Mills & Boon
the rose of romance

AND THEN HE KISSED HER...

This is the title of our new venture — an audio tape designed to help you become a successful Mills & Boon author!

In the past, those of you who asked us for advice on how to write for Mills & Boon have been supplied with brief printed guidelines. Our new tape expands on these and, by carefully chosen examples, shows you how to make your story come alive. And we think you'll enjoy listening to it.

You can still get the printed guidelines by writing to our Editorial Department. But, if you would like to have the tape, please send a cheque or postal order for £2.95 (which includes VAT and postage) to:

AND THEN HE KISSED HER...

To: Mills & Boon Reader Service, FREEPOST, P.O. Box 236, Croydon, Surrey CR9 9EL.

Please send me _____ copies of the audio tape. I enclose a cheque/postal order*, crossed and made payable to Mills & Boon Reader Service, for the sum of £_____.

*Please delete whichever is not applicable.

Signature _____

Name (BLOCK LETTERS) _____

Address _____

_____ Post Code _____